THE OUTER SPACE MYSTERY PIZZA CLUB

ELVIS IS MISSING

by Bruce Hale

illustrated by Luke Séguin-Magee

Penguin Workshop

To Kristina Replogle De Heras,
for all you do for SB kids—BH

For Phoebe and Marie,
my fantastic Grandmothers—LSM

PENGUIN WORKSHOP
An imprint of Penguin Random House LLC, New York

First published in the United States of America by Penguin Workshop,
an imprint of Penguin Random House LLC, New York, 2024

Text copyright © 2024 by Bruce Hale
Illustrations copyright © 2024 by Luke Séguin-Magee

Penguin supports copyright. Copyright fuels creativity, encourages diverse voices, promotes free speech, and creates a vibrant culture. Thank you for buying an authorized edition of this book and for complying with copyright laws by not reproducing, scanning, or distributing any part of it in any form without permission. You are supporting writers and allowing Penguin to continue to publish books for every reader.

PENGUIN is a registered trademark and PENGUIN WORKSHOP is a trademark of Penguin Books Ltd, and the W colophon is a registered trademark of Penguin Random House LLC.

Visit us online at penguinrandomhouse.com.

Library of Congress Cataloging-in-Publication Data is available.

Printed in the United States of America

ISBN 9780593660171

2nd Printing

LSCC

Design by Jay Emmanuel

This book is a work of fiction. Any references to historical events, real people, or real places are used fictitiously. Other names, characters, places, and events are products of the author's imagination, and any resemblance to actual events or places or persons, living or dead, is entirely coincidental.

The publisher does not have any control over and does not assume any responsibility for author or third-party websites or their content.

Chapter 1

STRANGER CRITTERS

Something was up. Elvis could tell.

Mr. and Mrs. Garcia-Jackson bustled about the house, dressed in their don't-jump-on-me clothes. House keys jangled, a sure sign of someone leaving. Jennica the Babysitter slouched in the armchair, half playing with her phone, half watching TV with Mateo and Valentina.

Anticipation curled through the room like the smoky scent of a distant fire.

Elvis whined. He paced across the kitchen tiles, toenails clicking.

Was the family planning to leave him alone with only a babysitter for company?

A hand reached down and scruffled his neck fur. "It's okay, buddy," said Mr. Garcia-Jackson. "The kids are staying home with you."

Elvis leaned into it. The scruffles felt good. But he still couldn't settle down.

Seeking more comfort, Elvis padded back into the family room and rested his chin on Mateo's knee. The boy didn't take his eyes off the screen. "Not now, pup," said Mateo. He patted Elvis twice and nudged his head away.

Elvis looked up at him with big eyes, but Mateo was oblivious.

Tina grabbed the remote from her brother. "It's almost on!"

Music swelled. Elvis glanced at the TV, but the swirling colors on the screen made his eyes feel strange. What was it with humans and their devices?

"Oooh, the Mystery Club, the Mystery Club / Cracking open mysteries is what we love!" Mateo and Tina sang along with the TV.

Jennica rolled her eyes, but the corners of her lips curled up. The older girl smelled calm and comforting, so Elvis trotted over and nose-bopped her. She scratched behind his ears.

"Any questions, any problems, we're just a phone call away," said Mrs. Garcia-Jackson. Fixing her earring, she glided into the room in a cloud of rose perfume.

"We know, Mom," Mateo and Tina chorused.

"Do what Jennica tells you."

"We will, Mom."

Mrs. Garcia-Jackson bent over the sofa to kiss each of them on the top of their heads. "And if any strangers knock at the door . . ."

"Don't let them in," the kids droned. But their eyes stayed glued to the screen.

Mrs. Garcia-Jackson lifted her purse from the side table. "There's a fire extinguisher by the back door, and a—"

"Honey, we'll miss our reservation," said Mr. Garcia-Jackson. He slipped an arm through hers.

"We'll be fine, Mrs. Garcia-Jackson," said Jennica. "Really." Elvis noticed the babysitter didn't roll her eyes this time, but she smelled like she wanted to. "Have fun!"

"Bye, kids!" their mother called as their father guided her out the door.

Tina and Mateo just grunted, absorbed by their TV show.

"Thought they'd never leave," Tina muttered after the door closed.

"Shh!" her brother shushed.

They focused on the screen.

Elvis sighed. He lay down with his chin on Jennica's foot. She'd taken care of him one time before, when the family went away for the weekend. Though he preferred his own humans, Elvis approved of her. The girl understood the importance of treats.

Before long, the dog caught a familiar scent. He raised his head, sniffing deeply. Sure enough, a few seconds later, someone rapped on the back door.

Elvis barked with great enthusiasm. Nobody was a better barker.

Rising, Mateo said, "I'll get it."

"What did your mom just say?" asked Jennica.

"No worries. It's only Booker."

Elvis lunged up to join the boy. Sure, he knew who was at the door, but what fun was being a watchdog if you couldn't bark?

Outside the back door stood a skinny boy about Mateo's age with poodle-curly hair.

"Where you been, Book?" asked Mateo.

"Dude, my gran made me triple-check my homework," said Booker. "She's mean. Not like your babysitter. Hi, Jennica!" he called.

"Hey, Booker," said the babysitter.

"You only missed the intro," said Mateo, flinging the door open wide. "Come on in."

And that was when Elvis caught it. A weird, wild scent. A scent he'd never smelled before. His nose lit up with the strangeness of it, and he stiffened, neck ruff bristling.

What was it?

Cat, but not a cat. Raccoon but not a raccoon. Some completely new critter?

Whatever it was, he'd teach it not to invade his territory.

"*Arrrr-ruff-ruff-ruff!*" With a savage bark, Elvis sprang through the open doorway, shoving Booker aside.

"Elvis, no!" cried Mateo.

"What's wrong?" Jennica asked.

"Elvis got out!"

Mateo and Booker took off running after the dog. Tina hopped off the sofa. "Let's go!"

"Won't they catch him?" Jennica asked, glancing up from her phone.

"You know about 'The Tortoise and the Hare'?"

"Yeah?"

Tina smirked. "Any turtle in tennis shoes could beat those two. Come on!"

The two girls dashed out the door. Responsible Jennica made sure to close it behind them.

Bluish twilight bathed the scene. The Garcia-Jacksons' backyard bumped up against wild parkland, with only a low fence separating it from the tangle of trees and bushes. Booker's place was right next door. By the time the girls reached the back fence, Booker and Mateo were disappearing into the trees.

"Elvis! Here, Elvis!" the boys called. Mateo scrubbed a hand over his face. Maybe if he'd paid the dog more attention, Elvis wouldn't have run off.

Between tree trunks, they glimpsed the dog up ahead. Elvis was bounding through the bushes, closing in on . . . something. *What the heck is that?* Mateo wondered.

Elvis wondered, too. He dimly heard the humans, but his nostrils were full of this raccoon-cat-whatever. He gained on the creature with every bound. Soon he'd show this pest a thing or two . . .

The critter dodged around a tree. Glancing back,

it spotted Elvis right on its bushy tail.

"*Ee-ee-ee-eek!*" the thing chittered. Elvis charged forward. But it zigged when he thought it would zag.

Fake out! He crashed into the bushes.

With a growl, the dog recovered. Once more, he galloped after the creature, ears flapping.

"Elvis, come!" one of the kids called. But Elvis ignored them. His blood was up.

Just ahead, two mighty oaks had fallen, forming a wide A that blocked the critter's path. Ha! The pest was headed straight for the middle of the A.

Now Elvis had it cornered. He put on a burst of speed.

But before he could reach the maddening creature, the air ahead rippled into a strange shape. Roughly oval, taller than a human. It was hard to tell in the twilight, but Elvis thought the shape twinkled, like the starry midnight sky.

With one last "Eee!" the creature jumped into the air . . .

And vanished.

Elvis snarled. No way was that pesky whatever-it-was making a fool of him. He leaped after it, disappearing into that circle of sparkles.

"Wh-where'd he go?" Mateo stuttered to a halt. He and Booker had arrived just in time to witness Elvis's back end disappearing into nothingness.

"I, uh . . ."

Both boys stared at that shimmering piece of night sky in the middle of the twilight woods.

It wasn't possible. Was it?

Jennica and Tina jogged up to join them. "Did you lose him?" asked Tina. She noticed that Mateo wore a weird expression on his face. Weirder than usual, anyway. "Where's Elvis?"

Her older brother just stared at the place where two fallen trees met.

"He, um, disappeared," said Booker.

"Into the bushes?" asked Jennica.

Mateo shook his head. "Into *that*." He pointed.

Fists on hips, Tina frowned at the glittering circle. "He went in there? Then let's get him out." As she stepped forward, Jennica caught her arm.

"Wait," said the babysitter. "We don't know what that is."

"So?" said Tina.

"Until we do, I don't want you getting any closer."

Slipping from Jennica's grip, Tina said, "We know that's where Elvis went. Good enough for me." She strode forward.

"Tina, stop!" said the babysitter. "Your parents—"

But Tina, as so often happened when she was with Jennica, wasn't listening. She marched into the circle calling, "Elvis!"

And vanished from sight.

"No way!" Jennica gasped. "She just . . ."

Mateo shifted from foot to foot. He wanted to follow his sister, but he couldn't help overthinking things. To go or not to go? He glanced at his friend. "It's like in those Narnia books."

"Yeah?" said Booker.

"It's a portal," said Mateo. "Think it's safe?"

"Definitely not."

"Wonder where it goes?"

Booker shrugged. "Someplace dark, deadly, and dangerous?"

"Don't even think about it," said Jennica.

Mateo bit his lip, staring into the void. "Still, she's my sister. We should . . ."

"I guess," said Booker. "Even though nothing good will come of it."

In her bossy babysitter voice, Jennica said, "I forbid you to go through."

Mateo sighed. Maybe he wasn't a hero like those in the stories he read. Maybe he was just some nobody who loved books and movies and pizza. But he couldn't let his younger sister and his dog face the unknown by themselves.

He stepped forward with Booker.

"Don't you dare!" Jennica snapped.

"Sorry," said Mateo. "But I've got to—"

"No!" Jennica crossed her arms. "Your parents trusted me to take care of you guys."

With a glance back, he said, "Then you'd better come along."

"Mateo . . ." Jennica's voice held a warning.

But he ignored her, just like his sister had. With a nervous flip of his stomach, Mateo stepped into the circle of starlight.

And the world turned inside out.

Chapter 2
COOLING WITH THE HOMERS

Sounds like crystal bowls chiming, swirls of rainbow light, smeared stars everywhere, the smell of incense. It was like the time Mateo had accidentally walked into that New Age store, but a thousand times more intense.

Now his insides felt like they were rearranging themselves. Mateo's brain and belly switched places. He was looking out of his ear holes and hearing out of his mouth. He was floating, flying, spinning . . .

And just like that, it was over.

Blinking against bright sunlight, Mateo found his feet touching down on some spongy surface. Then instantly he was airborne again. Had he landed on a trampoline?

Tears streamed down his cheeks as he fought to clear his vision. Mateo's nostrils flared at the scent of some strange perfume, and then his feet hit solid ground again. This time he bent his knees to stay low.

It helped. After two short bounces, he was finally able to keep his feet planted.

Mateo opened his eyes fully.

And his jaw dropped.

He wasn't on Earth. Or Middle-earth. Or anywhere he'd ever heard of.

For one thing, the sky was lavender. Lavender, like jacaranda flowers. And two suns shone in it—a big one and its little brother. Bringing his gaze downward, Mateo saw twisted lemon-yellow and burnt-orange trees straight from a Dr. Seuss book growing by a grassy meadow the color of his oldest blue jeans. Closer at hand, a fence encircled the portal.

At a sound from behind, he whirled. Booker's arms and legs pinwheeled as he descended through the air. And then, Jennica popped into sight.

Mateo rocked back on his heels. His breath huffed out in surprise. Where in the world were they?

The air was breathable, but it smelled funny. Like old-lady perfume mixed with orange blossoms and moo shu pork.

Landing nearby, Booker squinted at Mateo. "Well, we're not dead. Yet."

"But we're not in Kansas anymore."

"Truth," said Booker. He took a normal step and bounded up into the air again. "Hate to say it, but I was right!"

"About what?" asked Mateo.

"It's dangerous." Booker drifted downward. "Low gravity, which means thinner air. We'll probably die of suffocation. Or maybe our blood will boil."

"Don't say that."

Booker scowled his usual scowl. "And if we don't suffocate, we'll probably go like one of the Star Trek away crew."

"You mean . . . ?"

"Eaten by some gross-looking space monster. It's only a matter of time."

Checking around them, Mateo didn't spot any

space monsters. Just a couple of curious teens outside the fence, and Jennica, who was going all bouncy-bouncy like he and Booker had.

"I don't see any aliens," said Mateo. "Only some regular high school kids. So maybe we're not on a different planet, just—"

"A parallel reality? Fairyland? It doesn't matter where," said Booker. "We're doomed."

By the time Jennica was able to get her movements under control and join them, Mateo was feeling light-headed. He had to find his sister and Elvis, but it was getting harder to think clearly.

"Anyone else feel dizzy?" he asked.

Jennica and Booker both nodded. She was staring wide-eyed at the world around them.

"Stay close, you guys," said Jennica. "We don't know if this place is safe."

"Oh, it's definitely not," said Booker.

Stopping just beyond the fence, the two teens called out a greeting. But to Mateo, their words sounded like, *"Norfluppa rangle dinka dook?"*

He shook his head. Was the lighter atmosphere messing with his hearing? "What did you say?" he asked.

At this, their faces lit up. "You speak Earth language!" said the boy.

"We too," said the girl. "We love Earth!"

Booker and Mateo exchanged a glance. These were aliens? They looked just like regular teens you'd see at the mall. The boy—at least, Mateo thought he was a boy—wore a T-shirt and pants, while his companion sported a colorful outfit like something from an old issue of *Teen Vogue*.

Turning half away from them, Mateo muttered to his buddy, "Hey, at least they're friendly."

"For now," said Booker.

With a tentative smile, Mateo asked the aliens, "So, um, you look human. What are you?"

"We're Rhunnin," said the boy.

Booker looked around with alarm. "Runnin' from what?"

"From Kroon, of course," said the girl.

Mateo's brain hurt. Were they using alien words, or was lack of oxygen confusing him?

Trying to approach the visitors, Jennica found herself leaping into the air like a kangaroo. "Whoa! Not used to your gravity yet," she said. "Uh, where are we?"

"This?" the boy said. "Only Boogbee City on planet Kroon, most awesome planet in Flooktar Nebula."

"We have very important question for you," said the girl.

"Okay," said Jennica.

"Did you bring Earth pizza?" the aliens chorused.

"No." Booker gave them a dubious look. "Why would you ask?"

Both aliens beamed. "We love Earth pizza! Most popular food on Kroon."

This statement inspired a whole host of questions.

But Mateo only wanted to know one thing. "Have you seen my sister?" he asked, cautiously approaching. "Or our dog?"

"Dog? No," said the girl.

A wave of dizziness struck Mateo, and he had to lean against the fence to keep from falling.

"Careful," said the other alien. "Here, chew on this." He fished a canister from his pocket, then shook a small blue triangle into Mateo's hand.

Jennica's eyebrow arched. She reached out to stop Mateo. "Hold on. What is that?"

"Goofaw gum," said the girl. "We chew it when gravity changes."

Booker frowned. "When gravity *changes*?"

"We gave some to the Earth girl who came through before you," said the other alien, passing gum to Jennica and Booker.

"My sister!" said Mateo.

His head cleared as he chewed. The gum tasted a little like an orangutan's armpit, but it really helped with his dizziness. Mateo couldn't help thinking of his dog. Poor Elvis. Nobody was giving *him* goofaw gum.

Now that he saw them close-up, Mateo had a hard time telling these alien teens from normal Earth teens. They wore regular clothes, had medium-brown skin, and slightly pointy ears. The girl's hair was dyed green and purple at the ends. Her friend sported swoopy boy-band hair and his T-shirt read: 'ZA!

"You and that other girl are my first Earthlings!" gushed the girl. "Happy to meet you. I am what you would call female. My name is Clorox."

"Big, big pleasure," said the other alien. "I'm a dude, dude. Call me NoWay."

Mateo didn't comment on the odd names. After all, he had a classmate who went by Scrumptious. The three Earthlings introduced themselves.

"I love your clothing style," said Clorox, fingering Jennica's blouse. "Very spotty."

"You mean *sporty*?" said NoWay.

Smiling at the compliment, the babysitter glanced down at herself. "This old thing?"

Mateo shifted from foot to foot. "Um, I don't want to be rude, but while we're yakking, my sister and our dog could be in terrible danger."

"Danger?" NoWay and Clorox burst out laughing. "Relax," said NoWay. "Kroon is safer than a wantoon's piggalilly."

The Earth kids stared at him blankly.

NoWay looked disappointed, like his joke hadn't landed. "In other words, perfectly safe."

Booker scowled. *"Perfectly?"*

"Well, except for the monsters," said Clorox.

"Monsters?!" Jennica put a hand to her chest.

"And the goo storms," said NoWay.

"Goo storms?" said Mateo.

"And the gravity shifts," said Clorox. "But I wouldn't worry."

Folding his arms, Booker said, "So what you're saying is, we're *all* in terrible danger."

NoWay shrugged. "You get used to it."

Jennica peered around her as if she expected all three calamities to happen at once. She told Booker and Mateo, "Let's find your sister and Elvis and get out of here ASAP."

NoWay cocked his head. "A sap? What means this?"

"It's an abbreviation," said Booker. "For . . . uh, you know what? Skip it."

Both alien teens skipped along the grass. "Like this?" called NoWay.

Mateo groaned.

Meeting the aliens had briefly taken his mind off why they were here, but once again the truth hit home: Elvis and Tina were out there somewhere, facing monsters and goo storms and who knew what else. His stomach did a quick somersault. Was he brave enough to ride to their rescue?

Ready or not, he had to try. Taking advantage of the low gravity, Mateo crouched down and jumped all the way over the fence.

"Where do you go?" asked Clorox.

"To find Tina and our dog," he said. "Which way?"

After exchanging a few words with Clorox in their own language, NoWay turned to Mateo. "We're coming, too," he said.

"You need guide," said Clorox. "Plus, I have always wanted to cool with Earth people."

"'Cool'?" asked Booker.

The alien girl frowned. "Is this not the right word? For when you spend time relaxing with homers?"

"Oh, you mean *chill*?" said Jennica. "Like with your *homies*?"

"Yes, yes!" said Clorox. "Chill with homies."

Booker shook his head. "Nobody says that anymore."

"Can we save the slang lesson for later?" asked Mateo. "Elvis could be in real trouble."

"Elvis, like singing Earth man?" asked Clorox.

"No, Elvis, like my dog," said Mateo.

"Okey dokey, artichokey," said Clorox.

Booker rolled his eyes. These aliens had a lot to learn about Earth slang. He and Jennica jumped over the fence and joined the others.

With a dramatic sweep of his arm, NoWay sang out, "Away we go—to infinity and beyond!"

Mateo didn't want infinity. He wanted to be home and safe, curled up on his couch. But his journey had only just begun.

And with that, the little party set out into strange territory and certain danger.

Chapter 3

CAPTAIN CRUNCH SAYS, DANCE!

The tree-filled area surrounding the portal turned out to be the heart of a Boogbee City park. As the alien teens guided them down a winding path, the Earthlings bounced along, taking enormous strides, and leaping tall bushes in a single bound.

Hey, just because they were worried about Elvis was no reason to miss out on the fun side of low gravity.

"Your sister went this way," said Clorox, taking the lead. "You know, if she changed her clothing choices, she could appear much more chiller."

"You mean *cooler*?" Booker chuckled. "Good luck telling Tina that."

"She was in such a hurry, she didn't even stay to talk pizza," said NoWay.

Jennica frowned at the floppy-haired boy. "Talk pizza? What is there to talk about?"

23

"Toppings, cheeses, and the most important question of all."

The babysitter smiled despite herself. "Which is?"

"Do you like thin crust or thick?"

"Tina!" Mateo called. "Where are you?"

Catching NoWay's attention, Booker said, "Hey, I've been wondering something."

"Yes?"

"The odds of meeting an alien race that speaks English are at least a billion to one," said Booker. "But you speak English. How come?"

In the middle of a leap, Clorox spun to face him. "Why, we watch your historical broadcasts. Of course."

"What do you mean?" asked Jennica.

Mateo called for his sister again. No answer.

"We intercepted broadcasts from your planet," NoWay explained. "All of Kroon is fascinated by stories from your history. That is how we learn your languages."

"Our history?" Booker repeated. "Like . . . ?"

"The story of the Mother of Dragons," said NoWay. "Or that poor yellow Simpson family."

"Or the one about those six friends who cannot get away from each other," said Clorox. "That is my favorite."

"But those are just TV shows," said Jennica.

"Yes, our scientists know all about your television," said NoWay. "Ingenious!"

"But they're not—" Booker began.

"Tina!" Mateo called again. And this time there was an answering cry. "Come on!" he told the others.

Weaving through more of those warped Dr. Seussian trees, the crew reached a wide clearing where groups of aliens sat on the blue grass eating and chatting. Picnicking, maybe? Some were very humanoid—Rhunnin?—like Clorox and NoWay. A few were shorter and stumpier, but still pretty human-looking. Off to the side, laughing aliens tossed some type of sphere back and forth.

"Look, baseball!" cried Booker.

"No," said Clorox. "Mookball."

"That's the name of the game?"

"Kind of," said NoWay. "The ball is made from the head of a mook."

"Eww, no way!" said Jennica.

"Yes?" said NoWay.

"Uh, never mind," said the babysitter.

Spotting his sister chatting with a group of picnickers, Mateo hurried over to her. When he arrived, Tina was thanking the family for their help.

"There you are," he said. "We were worried."

She glanced up at her brother. "Took you long enough."

"You can't just run off like that," said Jennica, joining them. "You could have been hurt or killed."

"But I wasn't," said Tina.

"You need to wait for us," said Jennica.

Tina smirked. "No, you guys need to keep up."

With an effort, Mateo suppressed his irritation. His sister specialized in annoying, but right now, they had bigger issues. "Any sign of Elvis?"

Indicating a nearby pond, Tina said, "That family told me Elvis chased a griblik through their picnic and into the water."

"A griblik?" asked Booker.

"Whatever weird thing Elvis saw in our backyard," said Tina.

The crew investigated the pond's muddy bank. "Paw prints!" said Mateo. "And it—"

"Looks like they passed through here and headed off that way," said Tina. On the far side, some trampled reeds and animal tracks told the story.

"I was just about to say that," Mateo grumbled.

"Beat you to it." She stopped just shy of sticking out her tongue.

As they skirted the pond and followed Elvis's muddy tracks, Tina said, "That family also told me somebody called Monster Control on him. What's that?"

NoWay and Clorox traded a look.

"What?" asked Mateo.

"They, um, take care of monsters that bother our people," said Clorox.

"But Elvis isn't a monster," said Tina, her face flushing. "He's our pet."

"I'm sure they'll realize that." Jennica patted Tina's shoulder.

She shook off the hand. "We've got to find him before they do. Move it!"

Watching Tina forge ahead, Mateo wished he was a little more like his sister. Sure, Tina often (okay, *usually*) acted without stopping to think, and sure, she was bossier than a marine drill sergeant in boot camp. But at least she made decisions and acted on them.

Mateo was different. Sometimes he felt like he was watching his own life as a spectator, never sure which choice to make.

Across the grass, the tracks led up to a sprawling kidney-shaped building. Disturbing noises, like a wounded water buffalo swallowing a saxophone, drifted out the half-open door.

Booker edged back. "Something's getting tortured. Let's not be next."

Rubbing the back of his neck, Mateo worried about Elvis. Were those aliens hurting him?

"You sure he went in there?" asked Jennica.

"Prints don't lie," said Tina, pushing the door farther open.

When the crew entered the structure, they found themselves in a domed chamber with about fifty aliens—both the short kind and the tall kind—clustered around a raised platform. On the stand, an older woman blew into a contraption that looked like the mutant baby of a microwave oven and a tuba.

She finished making the ear-punishing noise and stood. Her audience responded with high-pitched keening and by slapping their thighs.

"Are they begging for mercy?" asked Booker.

"It's a, how do you say, contest of abilities?" said NoWay.

Jennica looked doubtful. "Talent contest?"

"Yes, that," said Clorox.

Going up on tiptoe, Tina scanned the room. "I don't see Elvis anywhere. Let's ask someone." She strode over to a man who looked similar to NoWay and Clorox, but with a golden hat, an electric-pink shirt, and an electronic notepad. "Hey, mister, have you seen our dog?"

Mr. Gold Hat beamed down at her. "Earth person! We very happy seeing you. Welcome to contest. Win pizza?"

Booker lifted an eyebrow. "Again with the pizza? What's the deal?"

"It is prize for contest," said Clorox.

"But pizza from Earth? How?"

"We get pizza from IGPDS," said NoWay, pointing at his T-shirt.

Squinting at the small type below the 'ZA!, Booker read: "Inter-Galactic Pizza Delivery Service?"

"Truly ronk-tiddley!" said Clorox and NoWay. "Every slice is nice!"

"We're not here for the contest," Mateo told Mr. Gold Hat. "We're looking for our dog. You know, dog?" He held a hand above the floor to indicate Elvis's size.

When Mr. Gold Hat frowned, Clorox stepped forward and said a few quick phrases in their language. He replied, and they went back and forth a couple of times. Finally, the alien girl turned to the Earthlings.

"Well?" asked Jennica. "What's up?"

"The sky, the clouds . . . ," NoWay began.

Tina cut him off. "She means, what did he say?"

"Oh," said NoWay.

Clorox offered a pained smile. "He did see your pet."

"Great," said Tina. "Where's Elvis?"

Clorox glanced at NoWay, who took up the story. "Captain Crunch will tell you," he said, nodding at the emcee. "But first, he wants something."

"Let me guess," said Booker. "A bowl of milk and a spoon?"

"If it's cash, we didn't exactly bring our wallets," said Mateo.

Spreading her hands, Clorox said, "He does not want Earth money."

"No?" said Jennica.

"He wants a dance."

The kids regarded each other in confusion. "A dance?" Mateo repeated.

"Captain Crunch says your visit is historic," said NoWay.

"So?" said Tina.

"You have heard traditional Rhunnin song from Kroon." Clorox indicated the older alien with the mutant tuba. "Captain Crunch says it is only fair that you share traditional Earth dance."

"For exchange of culture," added NoWay.

Crossing his arms, Booker said, "And if we say no?"

NoWay shrugged. "Then he will not tell where dog went."

The Earth kids huddled. Tina thought they were wasting time, Mateo and Jennica felt they could use all the help they could get. And Booker?

"There *is* no traditional Earth dance that everyone knows," he said. "I can't believe I'm asking this, but what dance would we even do?"

"The floss?" said Mateo.

"Gangnam Style?" said Jennica.

Tina closed her eyes, then shook her head. She sighed heavily. "No," she said, "I know exactly what dance to do."

Chapter 4

BUS, STOPPED

As the most coordinated of the group, Jennica and Tina were elected to lead the dance. The four Earthlings stood on the raised platform, shifting uncomfortably as the crowd stared. Jennica took a deep breath. She'd been hoping for some easy babysitting money to help fund her volleyball team's trip. Visiting an alien planet had not been part of her evening's plans.

Floppy-haired NoWay flashed her a double thumbs-up. He was kind of cute. For an alien.

Jennica cleared her throat and then addressed the crowd. "Uh, greetings from planet Earth."

Clorox translated. The aliens all raised their hands, fingers spread wide, and shook them. Jennica guessed that jazz hands was their way to say *howdy*.

"Our, um, traditional dance requires audience participation," said Tina. "So follow us and dance. Ready?"

In ragged voices, the quartet sang:

*You put your left foot in, you put your left foot out.
You put your left foot in, and then you shake it all about...*

Dying of embarrassment, Mateo stumbled through the steps with the others. To his amazement, the Kroonians joined right in, shaking themselves all about and generally doing the Hokey Pokey like they had been born to do it.

When the kids finished, the crowd keened like a bunch of banshees, slapping their thighs with enthusiasm. Mateo hopped offstage and ran up to Captain Crunch.

"Marvelous!" crowed the man in the gold hat. "Truly *ronk-tiddley!*"

Mateo frowned in confusion.

"That is a good thing," said Clorox, joining them.

"Um, thanks, I guess," said Mateo. "Now tell us where our dog went?"

Since Captain Crunch didn't speak as much English as the alien teens, he told Clorox and NoWay the story, and they translated.

It seemed that Elvis had chased the griblik into the building. Right across the stage they ran, disrupting a floogen-boogen dance and eliminating the dancers from the contest.

That's my Elvis, thought Mateo.

"Very *not* ronk-tiddley!" the gold-hatted alien observed.

Captain Crunch had helped chase the creatures

out, Clorox said, and he was glad to see the last of them.

"That's it?!" Tina snapped. "I can't believe we did that stupid dance for nothing!"

"Does he have any clue where Elvis might have gone?" asked Mateo. "Anything at all?"

After a quick back-and-forth with Captain Crunch, NoWay reported, "Your dog chased the griblik onto a hover-bus, and it flew away."

"The griblik can fly?" asked Booker.

"No, the hover-bus," said NoWay.

"Then what are we waiting for?" said Tina. "Let's go catch it!"

And with that, she pushed through the crowd waiting to congratulate them and crossed to the back door. Mateo and the rest followed behind, fending off compliments as politely as possible.

The building's backside faced a broad avenue that edged the park. Pedestrians, both Rhunnin and the shorter race (whatever that was), strolled with strange creatures on leashes. Smaller hovercraft glided past above them.

Mateo glanced both ways but saw no hover-bus. "Now what?" he asked.

"Buses usually drive that way." Clorox pointed to the left.

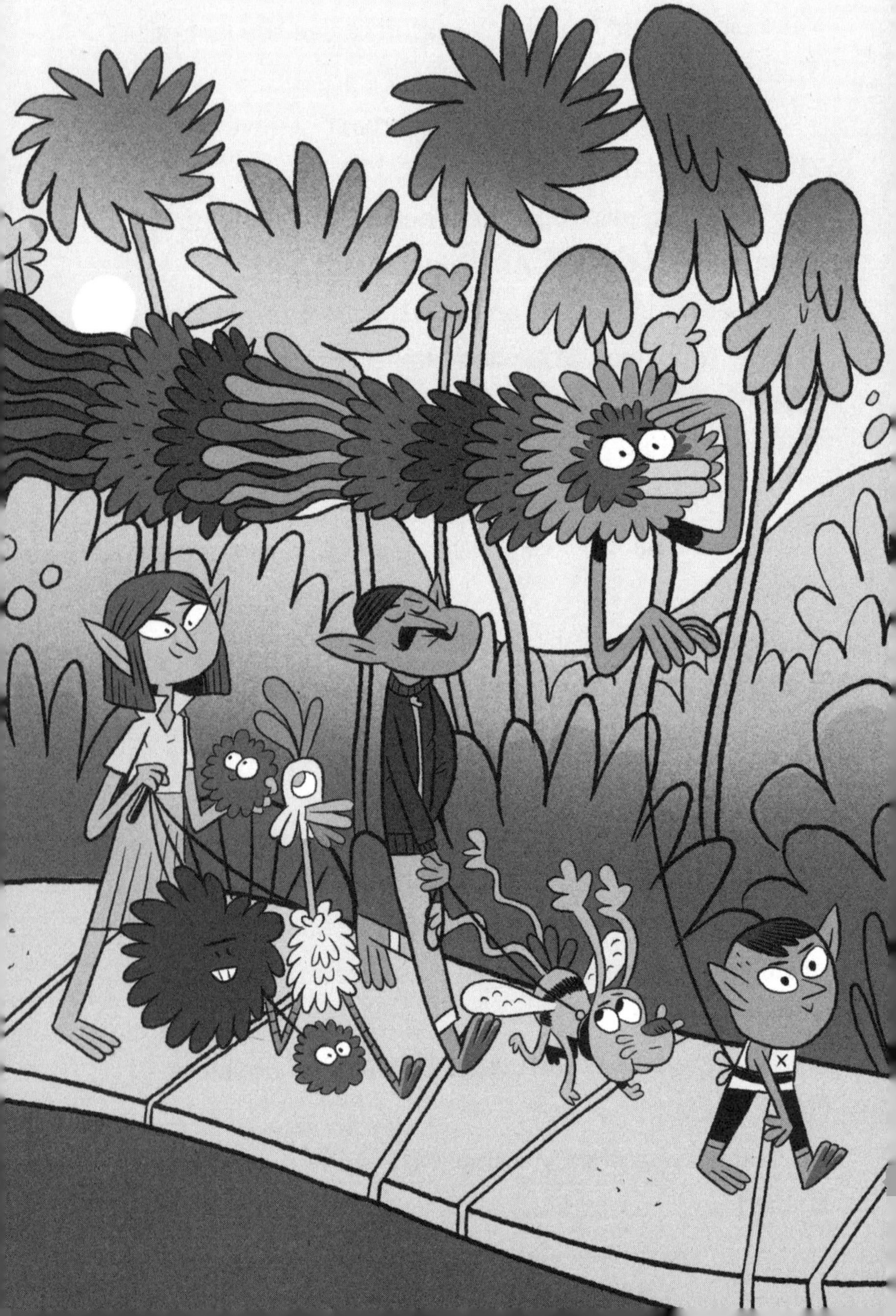

"Good enough for me." Mateo bounded along the sidewalk, dodging families, couples, and their pets.

"You know we can't outrun a bus," said Booker, just behind him. "Especially a flying bus."

Tina shot him a look. "You got any better ideas?"

"Like, don't take a portal into an alien world?" said Booker.

Casting a worried look at the strangeness surrounding them, Jennica caught up with NoWay. "Tell me something."

"Anything," said NoWay.

"Does time move at the same pace here as on Earth?"

The boy lifted a shoulder.

"It's just, we need to find this dog and get home as quickly as possible."

NoWay nodded. "Then let's hurry!"

Leaping along in low gravity, the crew kept their eyes peeled for any sign of Elvis or buses. After a few minutes of this, they spotted a knot of bystanders ahead, staring at something.

"You don't suppose . . . ?" Jennica asked.

Mateo raised his eyebrows. "That Elvis has something to do with that?"

When the group reached them, they found that the aliens were staring up at a bus.

In a tree.

"Oh, yeah," said Booker. "That's totally Elvis."

The last of the passengers were jumping down from the branches. Tina approached a man in a purple uniform and horned cap, who looked like he might be a bus driver.

"Hey, have you seen our dog?" she asked.

He spun, amazed. "Earth person?"

"Yeah, yeah, yeah," said Tina. "We're historic, I know. But have you seen our dog?"

NoWay described Elvis to the driver. The man's eyebrows drew down, and he spewed a stream of words in his alien tongue, growing ever louder as he gestured wildly.

The Earth kids stepped back.

"Yup, he's met Elvis," said Booker.

Mateo held up his hands, palms out. "We're sorry," he said. "Elvis means well, but he needs more training."

The driver kept up his tirade, jabbing a finger at the bus in the tree. Clorox tried to calm him down while NoWay translated.

"Your dog chased griblik onto bus as it was leaving," said the alien teen. "They ran around bus, then griblik climbed onto driver's head."

The man in purple indicated the angry red welts

on his cheek from the creature's claws. Mateo winced in sympathy.

"And then what happened?" asked Tina.

Clorox shrugged. "You can guess. Driver lost control; bus went *ba-sploish!*"

Glancing around, Mateo asked, "So where's Elvis?"

"Was he hurt?" asked Tina, biting her fingernail.

When NoWay translated their questions, the driver snarled a string of what Mateo suspected might be Kroonian curse words. *"Rebblar!"* he spat. *"Ta, tanka royla bushaka."*

At this, the alien teens exchanged a solemn look.

"What?" asked Jennica. "What aren't you telling us?"

Clamping his lips together, NoWay nudged Clorox. "It's . . . Monster Control," she said reluctantly. "They took away dog and griblik."

"W-what will happen to them?" asked Mateo.

Tina clasped her hands. "They won't put Elvis to sleep, will they?"

The alien teens chuckled. "To sleep? No, no, no," said Clorox. "Never."

Sagging in relief, the Earth kids smiled at each other. "Well, that's good," said Tina.

"But they might kill him," said NoWay.

"What?!" squawked Mateo.

His legs felt weak. A sudden coldness pierced him to the core.

Grabbing a fistful of NoWay's T-shirt, Tina hauled him closer. "Take us to Monster Control, Star Boy," she snarled. "And step on it!"

When NoWay opened his mouth to comment, Tina growled, "Not. One. Word."

NoWay nodded, and off they went.

Chapter 5

FACING MRS. FROWNYPANTS

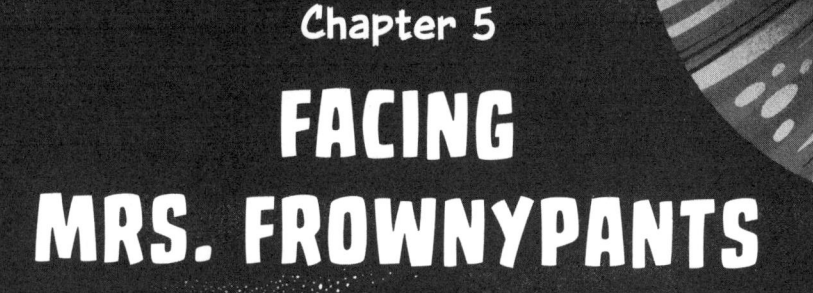

Monster Control's office was every bit as delightful and cheery as you'd expect from a place with that name. The dark gray building squatted, as wide and ugly as a cane toad, on a rundown-looking stretch of the avenue. Trash surrounded it. Someone had painted a mural on one wall to brighten things up. It didn't help.

The nightmarish shapes of various monsters—all claws, fangs, and horns in Day-Glo colors—leered down at passersby.

"Lovely," said Booker. "A real vacation spot."

Thanks to lots of leaping in low gravity, they had arrived in record time. But would they be quick enough to save Elvis?

Tina hammered on what looked like a door. No reply.

Mateo's stomach tied itself into a square knot.

Then Clorox pushed a green button on the wall. The screen above it lit up, revealing a grumpy female face that reminded Mateo of every unhelpful store clerk he'd ever met. With NoWay's assistance, Clorox explained their situation.

Mrs. Frownypants looked the crew over, unimpressed. She addressed the alien teens.

"We have missed visiting hours," Clorox translated.

The Rhunnin Monster Control worker spat out a few more phrases. "She says, come back tomorrow," NoWay translated.

"Tomorrow?!" cried Mateo, his heart sinking into his socks. "No way!"

"Yes?" said NoWay.

"Never mind," said Booker.

"Uh-uh." Tina's eyes narrowed as she leaned closer

to the screen. "Listen up, lady. You let us in right now!"

At this, the clerk's eyes widened. "Earth persons?"

"Duh!" said the four Earth kids.

Mrs. Frownypants blurted a quick question to the alien teens.

"She asks, did you bring pizza?" said Clorox.

Tina threw up her hands. "Not a slice! Now let us in!"

After NoWay translated the English words, the alien clerk stroked her nose.

"Well?" Tina demanded.

"She is thinking," said Clorox. At last, Mrs. Frownypants spoke, and Clorox conveyed her message. "She will let us in—"

"Great!" said Mateo.

"—if you will all do face plant," the girl finished.

The Earth kids frowned at each other. "Face plant?" asked Jennica. "Like falling face down onto something?"

"No, it's . . . oh, *yush*." NoWay grimaced. "Easier to show you."

With that, part of the wall slid aside, and the crew stepped into Monster Control's entryway. Mateo thought it looked like a corridor in the starship *Enterprise*, all sleek metal and futuristic design. The short hallway led to a tall podium.

Behind it sat Mrs. Frownypants, now wearing a toothy expression that would have wilted houseplants. Mateo supposed it resembled a smile. Her gray-blue hair was done up in four buns, making her head look like the steering wheel of an old-timey sailing ship.

The clerk and the alien teens exchanged jazz-hand greetings. "*Nateetha wah-wah-go*, Earth persons!" said Mrs. Frownypants.

"Um, hi there," said Jennica.

Noticing several corridors radiating out behind the podium, Tina arched an eyebrow. She elbowed NoWay. "Ask her where the little girls' room is?"

The boy frowned. "On Kroon, little girls are not monsters. You won't find them here."

Tina smacked a palm against her forehead.

"No, she means the toilet, the bathroom, the potty," said Booker.

Recognition dawned on NoWay's face. "Ah, the *noop-noop*." He asked Mrs. Frownypants, who indicated one of the hallways.

"Back in a flash," said Tina, taking off.

"What flash?" Clorox searched for a bright light but saw nothing.

Mateo was tempted to accompany his sister, who definitely wasn't headed for the bathroom. But before he could move, the clerk bustled out from behind her podium, ushering him, Booker, and Jennica over to a plant-filled alcove. Gesturing at the row of violet-colored plants, Mrs. Frownypants issued her instructions.

"She wants you to put your face into bush," said Clorox.

Jennica grimaced. "Eww. Really?"

"Do we have to?" said Booker.

NoWay nodded. "It's the, how you say, price of nutrition?"

"Price of admission?" suggested Jennica.

"Yeah, that."

Though his heart hammered, Mateo stepped up. If this was the only way to save his dog, he wouldn't chicken out. "I'll go first," he said.

Putting a hand on his arm, Jennica said, "No, I'm your babysitter. Me first." Teeth gritted, she approached the plant. When her nose was just inches away, the violet plant reached out four of its broad leaves and wrapped them around her face.

"Yikes!" Jennica squealed.

"Hold still," said Clorox.

A short while later, the shrub released her. Jennica backed away, wiping a forearm across her face.

Mateo went next. It felt weird, but the plant was gentle.

Waiting until last, Booker grumbled, "That can't be sanitary. We'll probably catch some alien face disease." Still, he went ahead and took his turn.

Soon, the three plants they'd touched unfurled to reveal bas-relief sculptures of their faces done up in leaves.

"Oh, that's not creepy," said Booker.

"Not at all," Mateo agreed.

But the clerk seemed happy with the result. At least, she slapped her thighs.

Jennica folded her arms. "Okay, we've done our part. Now bring us Elvis."

With Mateo's help, NoWay described the dog to Mrs. Frownypants. The woman hustled back to her podium and spoke a few words into a tube. Her touch screen flashed a series of images. After checking each one, Mrs. Frownypants turned to Clorox and grunted a few words.

"He is gone," said the girl.

"Gone?" Mateo cried. "We're too late!"

It felt like someone had dropped a sandbag on his head. How could this be? Images of Elvis playing and running sprang to his mind. His dog had been so sweet, so goofy, so full of life. And now these crummy aliens had put him to sleep?

Mateo swayed, trying to catch his breath.

Just then, a panting Tina jogged up to them from a different corridor. "He's not here," she told her brother. "I searched the place."

Mateo's lip trembled. Pointing at Mrs. Frownypants, he said, "She says he's gone."

Tina clutched his arm. "No. That can't be." They collapsed onto a nearby bench.

"H-he was alive and happy j-just an hour ago," said Mateo. His throat clamped tight, and his eyes stung.

"I take back e-every mean thing I ever s-said about him," said Tina, choking on her words.

Booker rested his hands on his friends' shoulders. "Poor old Elvis."

Cocking her head, Clorox asked, "Something is wrong?"

Booker shot her a dirty look. "Oh, you think?"

"All the time," said the alien teen.

"She killed our dog!" Mateo burst out, tears oozing from his eyes. Tina buried her face in her hands.

"*Killed?*" asked NoWay.

He rattled off a question to Mrs. Frownypants, who appeared concerned at the Earth kids' reactions. They exchanged a few more words. Then the clerk's lips tightened, and she glanced around to make sure they were alone. At last she spoke in a low voice.

Clorox translated. "Not dead-gone, just gone-gone."

"Excuse me?" asked Jennica.

"She says sometimes rich collectors will pay for rare monster."

"Is that legal?"

Clorox lifted a shoulder.

"Wait, so you're saying Elvis *isn't* dead?" asked Mateo. Hope expanded inside him like a birthday balloon.

"Where did he go?" said Tina. "Who's got him?"

NoWay put the question to Mrs. Frownypants. The woman sucked air through her teeth, squinched up her face, and reluctantly answered.

"This clerk does not know," said Clorox, "and the other workers would never confess, but . . ."

"But?" Mateo prompted.

"The three major monster collectors are Nyquil, Nintendo, and Boola-Boola." Clorox turned up her palms. "Any one of them could have dog."

Jennica fought back a smile. "Interesting names."

Clapping her hands together, Tina said, "What are we waiting for? Let's pay these guys a visit."

"Before one of them decides they want doggy stew," muttered Booker darkly.

Tina blanched. Mateo shook his head. "Book, you're always a ray of sunshine," he said.

"I try," said Booker. "Lord knows I try."

Chapter 6
A SUGARY RIDE

As it happened, Nintendo was the closest of the monster collectors. She lived outside of town with her own private zoo. Time was slipping by. Since it was too far to walk, even in low gravity, the crew hustled off to NoWay's house to borrow his parents' hovercraft.

Mateo wished they could go even faster. As they bounded along the sidewalk past alien houses shaped like mushrooms, triangles, and Coke bottles, he tried to quiet that inner voice that said they might already be too late. Mateo bit his lip. What strange things would these rich aliens do to a poor dog from another planet?

Jennica kept checking her phone, but its clock didn't seem to work here. Who knew what time it was on Earth? Since they were moving as quickly as possible, she took the chance to satisfy her curiosity about Kroon.

"How come so many Kroonians have names from Earth?" she asked the Rhunnin teens.

Clorox grinned. "Almost half my life, we have watched historical broadcasts from your planet. Earth culture is very popular. That is why we copy your fashion."

"Ah, that explains the T-shirts and jeans."

"And Earth names are . . . exotic," said Clorox. "So many people take new Earth name."

"What's your real name?" asked Jennica.

"Rinkoid Tazoofa Lulululu," said Clorox. "But I thought Clorox sounded prettier."

Tina smirked.

"And what's with the pizza obsession?" asked Mateo, hoping to take his mind off Elvis's fate.

"Mmm, pizza!" the alien teens chorused. "Who doesn't love pizza?"

"Nobody I know," said Jennica.

NoWay explained. "Inter-Galactic Delivery Service brings us things from around the galaxy. Powdered snooft horns from Remulak."

"Zimbeezi juice from Outer Kreplock," Clorox added. "Very ronk-tiddley!"

"But when they introduced us to Earth pizza, that was that."

Clorox nodded. "Everybody wanted some. So they

made portal to Earth, and IGDS became IGPDS—pizza delivery only."

With a dreamy look, NoWay crooned, "The melty cheese, the chewy bread . . ."

"We need pizza!" cried Clorox.

Booker's stomach rumbled. It must have been dinnertime back home, and he was well past hungry. "Yeah, a slice would really hit the spot."

"Which spot?" Clorox glanced around them.

Booker shot her a look. "The empty spot in my belly."

When they reached a dome-shaped house, NoWay stopped them. "We're here."

"Where's the hover-car?" asked Tina.

"Yeah, let's get going," said Mateo.

The alien boy chided them. "Ah-ah-ah, pizza first."

Tina and Mateo grumbled, but they eventually gave in. No sense performing a daring rescue on an empty stomach.

Inside NoWay's house, the Earth kids marveled at the spongy floor and the furniture in geometric shapes. NoWay inserted a flash-frozen pizza into a wall slot. After a minute, something went *beep-bop-boop*, and the pizza slid back out on a tray, piping hot and smelling amazing.

"Smells like it's from Pizzageddon," said Jennica.

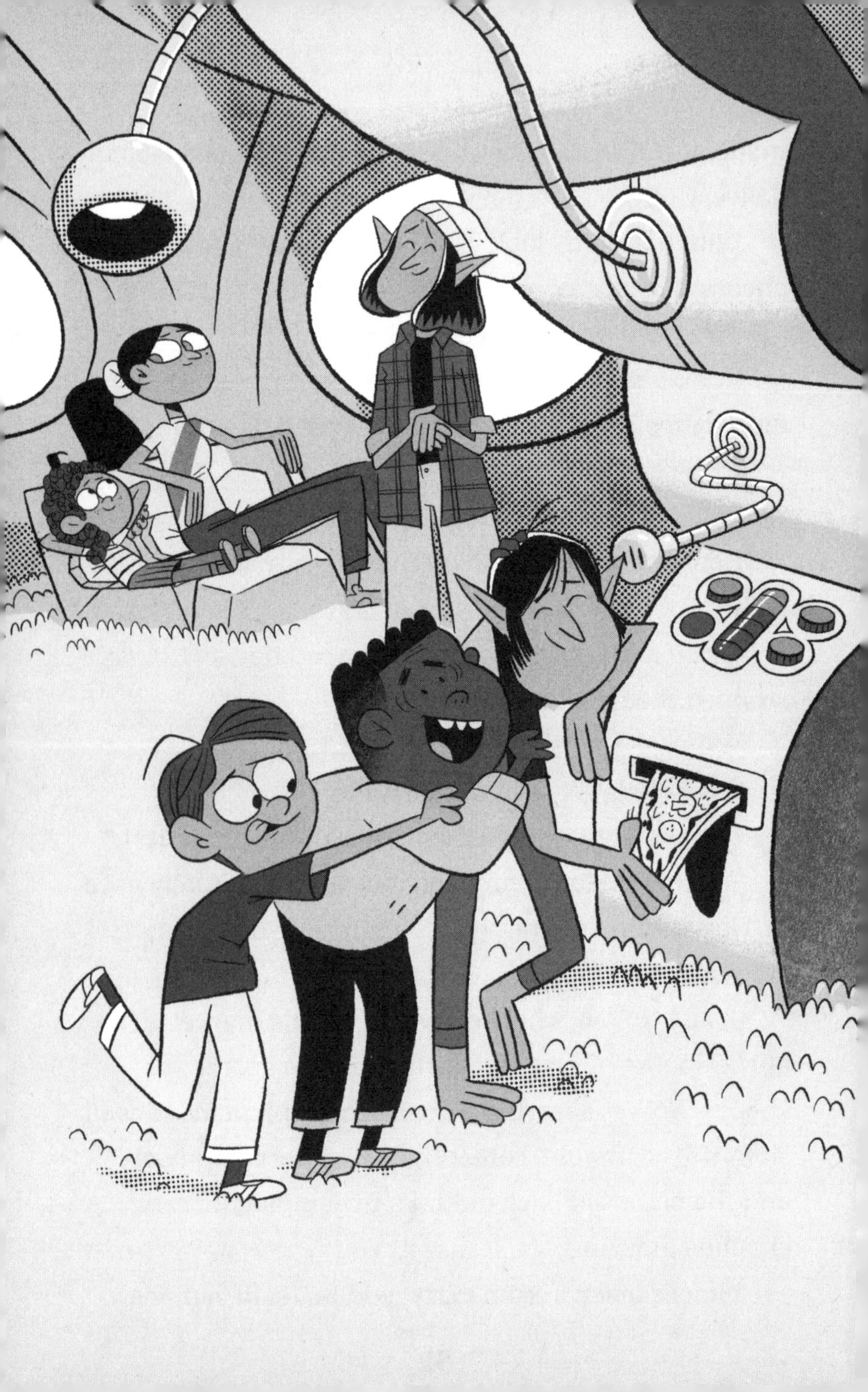

"The best in the galaxy!" cried the alien teens. "Pizza song!" And with that, they burst out singing:

Ohhh, a slice so nice that you wanna eat it twice!
Pizza, pizza!
Pineapple or pepperoni, everything except spumoni.
Pizza, pizza!

Mateo couldn't argue with them there. The crew fell on the hot pizza like starving wolverines on a deer carcass. In less time than it takes to tell, the pie was gone.

Booker ripped out a resonant belch.

"I couldn't agree more," said Mateo. "Now, where's that hovercraft?"

Leading the gang through the rainbow-colored rooms of his house, NoWay stopped in what Mateo assumed must be a garage. Mysterious tools hung on one wall, metal boxes lined another, and in the middle perched a lovely oval craft shaped something like a British driving cap.

One thing Mateo didn't see was a garage door.

"What do you think?" asked NoWay. "A sugary ride, eh?"

"Pretty sweet," said Mateo. "But, um, how do we get it outside?"

In answer, NoWay pushed a button on the wall. With a low hum, part of the roof rolled back, revealing the lavender sky. He lifted a key fob off a hook, squeezed it, and the top of the craft opened to reveal two bucket seats with a wide, curved bench seat behind them.

Jennica glanced at NoWay and fiddled with her hair. "Can I ride up front with you?"

"Certainly," said the alien boy with a wide smile.

Tina noticed that Clorox's eyes narrowed, but the girl joined the others on the rear bench without complaint. When NoWay inserted his key fob into the dashboard, the vehicle's roof slid back into place and the touch screen controls lit up.

Patting the dash, NoWay told the babysitter, "It's got the latest Zu-Mag drive. This baby can fly all the way up to *glork* level."

Lightly touching his forearm, Jennica widened her eyes. "Is that very high?"

"About sixty of your Earth feet."

"Oh my," said Jennica.

In the back seat, Clorox rolled her eyes. Some gestures were universal. "Do you even have driving permit yet?" she asked NoWay.

He flapped a hand. "Done everything but final test. Relax."

Clorox crossed her arms over her chest.

NoWay's hands danced across the dashboard, pressing here, stroking there. With a low whoosh, the hovercraft rose straight up through the hole in the roof. The portal closed beneath them.

"See?" said NoWay. "Nothing to it. Now, let's make like tree and split!"

"Leaf," corrected Booker.

"Leafing now!" cried the alien boy. He jerked the joystick all the way back, and the hovercraft rocketed into the sky. *"Yush!"*

"Not so high!" yelped Clorox.

"Sorry," said NoWay. He reversed the joystick, plunging the craft straight at the ground.

"Aaagh!" the Earth kids screamed.

The vehicle wobbled from side to side as it dove. "Sorry, sorry!" said NoWay. "Forgot to turn on stabilizers."

After a few more bumps, the hovercraft finally leveled out about ten feet above the avenue. Booker released his death grip on Mateo's knee.

"Looks like I'll finally achieve my life's ambition," he said.

"What's that?" asked Mateo.

"To die screaming on an alien planet."

To say the rest of the ride was a bumpy one would be like calling the Grand Canyon a little hole in the ground. Accurate, but a slight understatement. The hovercraft plowed through tree branches, terrorized a flock of flying critters, and very nearly decapitated a statue of some important Kroonian. Courting disaster, they made their way across the city.

By some small miracle, NoWay eventually landed the craft without crashing on a level area beside a series of enormous domed structures. Everyone sagged in relief.

"And here we are," said NoWay. "Easy-greasy, shaka-beezy."

"You sure your parents are okay with you borrowing this?" asked Mateo after he'd caught his breath. As soon as the roof slid back, he and the other passengers scrambled out onto solid ground.

"All is fine," said NoWay, buffing out a scratch in the paint with his T-shirt sleeve. "Parental units don't need to know."

Clorox led them, bounding down a winding path that approached the main dome.

But before they could reach it, a Klaxon blared a series of descending tones: *Toom, toom, toom!*

"Come close!" yelped Clorox.

"Why, what's the big deal?" said Tina.

Fishing the goofaw gum canister from his pocket, NoWay said, "Gravity is changing." He held out the container. Mateo tried walking over to him, but with every step, his legs felt harder and harder to lift, like he was wading through thickening concrete. A weight like a great invisible hand pressed down, doubling him over. His head ached with every heartbeat.

"It's . . . heavy," grunted Booker. He dropped to his knees.

"Too . . . heavy," said Jennica, who was already crawling.

Somehow the Earth kids reached NoWay, who handed them each a chunk of the gum. They lay there chewing, unable to move. Gradually, Mateo's headache faded. But he still felt bad.

"Book, I'm sorry I dragged you into all this," he said. "It's not your dog."

Booker patted his arm. "Friends stick together," he said. "Besides, how often does a guy get the chance to face death and disaster on an alien planet?"

After another minute or so, the Klaxon sounded again, this time on a rising tone. Slowly, slowly, the weight lifted. Everyone was able to stand again. Mateo noticed that the gravity now felt a lot like Earth's but lighter.

"Let's get going and search this zoo," said Jennica. "We've wasted enough time."

Working a kink out of her back, Tina said, "But how will we get inside? This is someone's home."

"Leave it to me," said Clorox. "I have idea."

Chapter 7
I OWE A LOT TO KAMAFLEEG SNOT

When they reached the front door, it slid open on its own. Just inside stood an enormous man in a blue-gray jumpsuit, with orange skin and two bumps on his forehead that looked like baby horns.

Clorox and NoWay greeted the man. He returned their greeting in a voice that rumbled like a landslide, while casting a suspicious eye on the Earth kids.

After a quick chat, Horned Orange nodded and ushered them inside. Raising a palm to signal the group to stay put, he then stomped out of the entryway and went deeper into the house.

"What did you tell him?" asked Mateo.

Clorox shrugged. "Just that you were important Earth persons who came long way to see Nintendo's Famous Zoo."

"Uh, that dude is orange," said Booker.

"Yup," said Mateo.

"That can't be healthy."

"He's a Pockadoo," said NoWay. "Very popular for security and heavy work."

"He's not Nintendo?" asked Jennica.

Clorox shook her head. "No, but he went to ask her if we can tour zoo."

Mateo jammed his hands into his pockets and paced through the entryway. He pictured Elvis in a comfortable cage, wagging his butt off at the sight of them. He hoped his unruly pooch was okay.

As they waited for the Pockadoo's return, Mateo heard a whuffling sound. He turned to see a squat animal scuttling along with its face to the floor, sucking up the dirt the group had tracked inside. All armored plates and thick, snuffly snout, it looked like the confused offspring of an armadillo, a turtle, and a warthog.

"Whoa!" said Jennica, catching sight of the thing. "What . . . ?"

"Hammina-jammina!" said NoWay. "She's got a glorkwhuffer? Aw, some people have all the luck."

"Um, glorkwhuffer?" asked Tina.

"They eat anything," said Clorox. "Rich people keep them to clean up around house."

Booker snorted. "How come they don't just *eat* the house?"

But before Clorox could explain, the Pockadoo returned with his mistress. Nintendo was a slim Rhunnin woman with high purple hair twisted into two huge pinwheels. Her simple clothes fit perfectly. Tina thought she resembled a Hollywood actress but couldn't think which one.

Nintendo spread her arms wide. "Earth visitors," she said, "welcome to my home!"

"Thank you," said Jennica. "We're uh, very excited to see your famous zoo."

The alien woman smiled. "Isn't everybody? It's the best."

She led them away from the entryway, through a living room big enough to host a regulation soccer game and all its fans, and into a tunnel pulsing with turquoise and mint-green lights.

"Would you like refreshment?" asked Nintendo.

Jennica lifted a shoulder. "Uh, sure."

The woman raised her arm, spoke into her ornate bracelet, and pressed two of its ruby-colored stones. When the group emerged from the tunnel into another dome, a short, scowling man was waiting with one tray of beverages and another of tiny pizza slices on toothpicks. Mateo gaped at the assistant's enormous nose and ears. The man resembled some of the short aliens he'd seen earlier.

"He is Nauga," Clorox whispered, taking a pizza slice. "Try not to stare."

After everyone had eaten a mini slice and taken a cup, Nintendo said, "Upward bottoms!" and downed her drink in one shot. The alien teens followed suit. Booker squinted suspiciously at his cup, but the other Earth kids drank down their refreshments.

It was sweet, Mateo thought. Like elderflower and honey, with a pinch of something he couldn't quite place. Very refreshing. "What is it?" he asked.

"Fresh kamazoo," said Nintendo.

Jennica's smile wavered. "And what's that?"

"Condensed sweat of zoomanka, mixed with kamafleeg mucus," said NoWay. "It's a rare treat."

The Earth kids went green. Booker set his cup back on the tray, untouched.

"We don't deserve your generosity," Mateo said.

"Nothing but best for my special guests," said Nintendo. "This way, please." With that, she sauntered up to an ornate archway and waved her bracelet past a scanner.

With a hiss like a soda can opening, a panel slid aside. Past Nintendo, Mateo glimpsed a row of glassed-in cages whose occupants sat up and stared at them. Tina sidled over, muttering, "If Elvis is here, how do we get him out?"

"We'll think of something," he whispered.

"You are impressed, yes?" Nintendo led them through the archway and into the zoo. "My collection is so famous, even Earth people know it?"

"Ah, yes," said Jennica. "It's the talk of the, uh, galaxy."

The Earth kids stared about them with growing wonder. It was like the weirder cast members of a Star Wars movie had all decided to room together. In the cages that ringed the dome, Mateo saw horned creatures, winged creatures, slime creatures, monsters with four eyes or three noses, and gloopy things with too many limbs, impossible to describe.

"You have heard of my nockatwee, of course," said Nintendo, with a lazy gesture at the nearest cage.

"Of course," said Booker. "It's the, uh, nocka-est."

Inside the enclosure squatted a big-eyed creature that resembled a hairball some giant cat had horked up. It blinked at the visitors, scuttling closer on a multitude of tiny feet.

"Uh," said Mateo, backing up.

"No other private zoos on Kroon have nockatwee." Nintendo sniffed. "Top that, Boola-Boola!"

Tina and Mateo kept scanning the cages as they toured, searching for Elvis. But no dogs appeared. Their host maintained a steady patter, showing off this monster and that one as they made their way through the dome.

"Do you have any, um, Earth monsters?" asked Mateo.

Nintendo spun to face him. "Why? Is one on Kroon?"

Biting his lip, Mateo wondered how much to tell her. Would this rich collector help them find a lost pet? Or would she try to keep it for her collection?

"Well, one of our, er, Earth monsters from our own, um, zoo escaped through the portal," said Mateo, making it up as he went. "And we'd really like to bring him back."

Tina elbowed him aside. "He's our pet dog," she

said. "And we're worried about him."

Nintendo's eyebrows lifted. "An Earth dog? That's no monster. I would never collect a higher life form like a dog. It is not proper."

"You got that right," said Tina.

Mateo slumped. Elvis wasn't here. They had struck out again. So far, their heroic rescue effort wasn't terribly heroic. Or successful.

Tapping her fingertips together, Nintendo uttered a long "Hmmm . . . If another collector has it, I will . . ." She tapped her bracelet, spoke a few words into it, and a voice answered in the alien tongue. After a rapid-fire conversation, their host lowered her arm.

"Well?" said Tina.

Nintendo's eyes narrowed. "Nokia does not have your dog—or so she says. And I would know if Boola-Boola captured it. My spy sees all."

"So what does that mean?" asked Mateo.

Stroking her nose for a long moment, Nintendo finally blurted, "Grunthar!"

"Gesundheit," said Jennica without thinking.

"What's Grunthar?" asked Booker.

NoWay spread his arms. "*Who's* Grunthar?"

"Yeah."

"Who's *Grunthar*?"

"That's what I said," said Booker.

"Former boy inventor and Earth expert," said Clorox. "NoWay admires him."

"He's kind of famous," said NoWay.

Cracking her knuckles, Tina said, "So this Grunter dude has Elvis? Let me at him."

"Sometimes things from Earth come through portal," said Nintendo. "Grunthar collects them."

"Okay," said Mateo. "Where does he live?"

Nintendo wobbled her head back and forth. "I can tell you where. But he is . . . different. Maybe he will meet you, maybe not."

"Can you put in a good word?" asked Jennica.

Nintendo's forehead crinkled. "Which word is good word? *Cheese? Pepperoni? Ronk-tiddley?*"

"No," said Mateo, "she means say good things about us."

The babysitter nodded. "It would help. We really need to go home soon."

At this, NoWay looked a little sad.

Nintendo nodded. "I will tell him to expect you."

With many thanks for the zoo tour and the kamafleeg snot, the crew hurried out to their waiting hovercraft. Just before they boarded, Clorox held out a hand to stop NoWay.

"What is it?" he asked.

"This time," she said, "I drive."

Chapter 8
CRATER COMFORTS

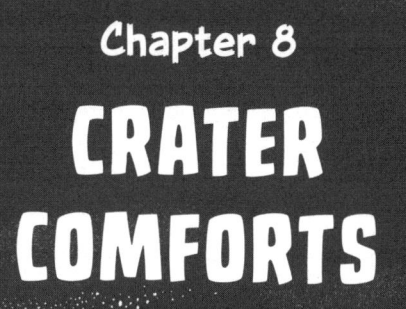

After a slightly less hair-raising trip through the Boogbee suburbs, Clorox piloted the hovercraft toward the strangest Kroonian house they'd seen so far. (And that was saying something.) Rising above the surrounding yellow and orange trees was a fake volcano the size of a quadruple-decker mega-mansion.

At least, they assumed it was fake.

"*That's* where he lives?" said Mateo.

"Dude's been watching too many James Bond movies," said Booker.

"No kidding."

Booker frowned. "You watch, it'll erupt on us."

Piloting the hovercraft around the lip of the structure, Clorox searched for a landing spot. "Where's the—?" she began.

As they cleared the lip, Mateo noticed the layer of fake magma below them was sliding to one side. Beneath it in the "crater" lay a landing pad where several other hovercrafts rested, as well as a fancy ornamental fountain.

Clorox managed to avoid hitting the fountain—she was a marginally better driver than NoWay—and they landed heavily without blood or tears being shed. Still, after Booker scrambled out, he asked, "Next time, can we just walk?"

Inside the volcano house, arched passageways lit in different colors branched out from the central crater. Above each arch hung a huge portrait of a scowling man with elephant ears and a big honker of a nose.

The paintings made him look like some kind of superhero. His muscles bulged. His gaze was noble. He looked ready to leap tall volcanoes in a single bound.

"I'm guessing that's Grunthar?" said Booker.

"Greatest of the great," sighed NoWay.

Tapping her foot, Jennica said, "Let's make it snappy with this guy. We don't know how late it's getting back home."

A sudden fanfare blasted. It sounded like a trumpet with a head cold.

From the blue archway, a short, squat man strode out to meet them, trailed by a Pockadoo and several Rhunnins. He was neither muscled nor noble.

"*That's* Grunthar?" muttered Booker. "I was expecting someone . . ."

"Taller?" whispered Tina.

"Buff-er?" murmured Mateo.

"Both," said Booker.

"Welcome to my humble dwelling," said the man, with a wide smile. "I am Grunthar the Great. No doubt you've heard of me?"

"Uh, sure," said Mateo. They'd heard about him from Nintendo, so this wasn't technically a lie.

"Splendid!" said the little man. Mateo noticed that Grunthar looked something like the Nauga assistant at Nintendo's zoo. That made at least three alien races on Kroon. He wondered how many more existed.

"We're looking for—" Tina began.

"Yes, yes," Grunthar interrupted. "Nintendo told me. I have never had Earth visitors before, so I hope you will let me show you around before we handle your business."

"Well, actually, we—" Jennica said.

"Wonderful! Let's go." After spinning on his heel, Grunthar marched off toward the pink archway. The crew had no choice but to follow along.

NoWay trotted up to the little man. "Such a pleasure to meet you in person," he said. "I am your idol."

Clorox poked him in the ribs.

"I mean, you are *my* idol." NoWay blushed. "All those amazing inventions—the TransMog Ray, the InvisiShield, the GravMod device—pure genius!"

Grunthar seemed to swell with pride like a bullfrog's throat. "Too true, too true."

"You're so awesome!"

"I can't deny it." The Nauga man swelled even more. Another compliment and Mateo thought he might pop.

"I can't wait to hear what amazing things you've invented lately," NoWay gushed.

A scowl darkened the inventor's face. "Nothing!" he snapped, deflating rapidly. "I'm *retired*!" And with that, Grunthar stomped ahead of the group.

One of the inventor's assistants pulled close and muttered, "The master is sensitive about that."

"Oh, you think?" said Booker.

"Yes, I do," said the assistant. "Every day."

Booker shook his head.

By this time, Grunthar had led them into an expansive hall. Fancy museum lighting illuminated objects displayed on a series of pedestals. When he turned to face the group, Grunthar's smile was back in place.

"I would be honored if you would inspect my prized collection of rare Earth objects," said the inventor.

With a quick glance, Tina scanned the exhibits. "A shoe, a shopping cart, a coffee maker, a tricycle, a dead squirrel, and a purple Frisbee."

"Hey," said Booker. "That's where it went."

"No offense, but we see these every day," said Tina. "So, where's our dog?"

NoWay gasped. "Tina!"

"What? That's why we're here."

"Grunthar is famous," said NoWay. "You shouldn't talk to him like that."

The inventor raised his palms. "It's true," he said. "I'm very famous and everyone should respect me. But this Earth girl is worried about her pet."

"Have you seen our dog?" asked Mateo. "Nintendo said people bring you things from Earth."

When Grunthar shook his head, his enormous ears flapped like a basset hound's. "So sad, but I have not seen your dog. I would love to meet one someday."

Tina and Mateo sagged. Time was running out. Elvis could be anywhere on this bizarre planet. They could search for days and never find him.

Mateo's eyes went misty. An image came to him of the time Elvis had chewed the stuffing out of his doggie bed and sat surrounded by foam chunks, wagging his tail like it was all a great game. A sad chuckle forced its way out.

"Any idea where to look?" asked Jennica. "We have to go home soon."

Grunthar began leading them back to the crater courtyard. "Kroon is a big planet. Not as big as Earth, but your dog could be anywhere."

Tina's lower lip quivered. Mateo's throat felt tight.

"But someone took Elvis from Monster Control," Booker said. "If not you or those other collectors, who else would want him?"

As they paced through the hallway, another glorkwhuffer waddled past in the opposite direction, sucking up dust bunnies. *Must be handy to have a staff of monsters*, Mateo thought absently. *Sure saves on salaries.*

Grunthar stroked his nose. "Hmm . . . there is someone. Pennzoil."

"The motor oil?" said Booker.

"The politician?" asked Clorox.

"Why would a politician want our dog?" said Mateo. "Elvis can't vote."

Just then, they passed by a room where several good-size monsters were hanging out. A hugely fat one that looked like a four-eyed elephant seal with wings just gave them a bored glance and returned to gnawing on its chew toy.

But another creature, one that resembled a cross between an ottoman-size beetle and a bunny rabbit, stared at the Earth kids. Emitting a high-pitched *woop-oop-oop* sound, it beelined for Mateo.

"Gah!" he cried, backing up.

"Don't worry," said Grunthar. "The foofaloofa is harmless."

"Who's worried?" Mateo attempted a chuckle as he backed into the wall behind him.

The foofaloofa just kept coming. Mateo braced himself. But the thing merely rubbed its rabbitlike head against him, as if it wanted to be petted.

Mateo gave it a couple of tentative pats. "Heh. Nice foofa?"

"Sorry." Grunthar dragged the creature back. "Hard to train a monster."

Clorox frowned. "I have never seen a foofaloofa act so friendly."

Shrugging, the inventor said, "It's more like a pet." He shoved the creature back into its room and closed the door. "Now, what was I saying?"

"Pennzoil," said NoWay.

"Yes, he's on the Earth Committee, so he might want your dog," said Grunthar. "Or . . ."

"Yes?" said Tina.

The inventor tugged on one of his long earlobes. "I hope this hasn't happened."

"What?" A jolt of alarm flashed down Mateo's spine.

"The Kwako Science Lab," said Grunthar. "They might have taken him for . . . experiments."

"Experiments?!" cried Tina. "Like cutting him open and stuff?"

"Indeed," said Grunthar.

"No way!"

"Yes?" said NoWay.

"Never mind!" cried Tina, Mateo, and Booker.

Tina took off running for their hovercraft. "Come on! We've got to stop those scientists."

The Earth kids and Clorox dashed after her. NoWay paused, turned to the inventor, and said, "It was such an honor to meet you."

"Yes, it was," said Grunthar. "For you."

Chapter 9

IT'S RAINING BROCCOLI

As they piled into the hovercraft willy-nilly, NoWay ended up in the driver's seat again.

"But I—" Clorox began.

"No time to switch," said Mateo.

"They could be operating on Elvis right now," said Tina. "Go, go, go!"

With a jerk and a wobble, the hovercraft rose through the volcano mansion's roof hatch and blasted off toward the city. Right away, it trimmed two treetops and nearly collided with a roof spire.

"Meepa-donka!" cried Clorox. "Stabilizers!"

"Right, right," said NoWay, engaging the controls.

Whipping along the broad thoroughfare about twenty feet off the ground, the hovercraft dodged around other vehicles. Or over them.

Mateo's head spun. Tina gripped the grab handle for dear life.

"Whoa," said Booker, clutching his stomach.

"Think I'm gonna toss my cookies."

"Please don't throw snacks," said NoWay. "This is my parental units' car."

With a groan, Booker said, "No, I mean upchuck. Vomit?"

Clorox's eyes grew round. "Oh. Use the woopsie bag." She indicated the airsickness sack hanging off NoWay's seat back.

A big intersection loomed before them.

"Which way?" asked NoWay.

Jennica's jaw dropped. "You're asking us?"

"Right! No, left!" cried Clorox.

Cranking the wheel hard to the left, NoWay simultaneously worked the joystick to dive under a slow-moving hover-van.

"I always get those two words confused," said Clorox.

Suddenly the hover-van moved, too—directly into their path.

"Look out!" yelled Mateo. Everyone screamed.

Gritting his teeth, Mateo watched events unfold as if in slow motion.

The van's rear end loomed large in their front window. NoWay tried to dive even lower. The van did, too. Then...

KRONCH!

They smacked into the vehicle. Even in the lighter gravity, the kids could feel the impact. Bodies jounced around inside their hovercraft.

WHOOMP!

Their vehicle hit the ground. Two seconds later, a load of softball-size green things rained down on NoWay's hood and windshield.

Mateo tensed into a knot, waiting for an explosion. Nothing happened.

He looked closer. "Is that . . . ?" he said.

"It can't be," said Tina.

"Broccoli?" asked Booker.

Clorox gasped. "Earth broccoli?"

"We just call it *broccoli*," said Booker. "The *Earth* part is understood."

"But," said NoWay.

All the color bled out of Clorox's face. "It is against law to import fruits and vegetables from Earth."

Craning their necks, Mateo and Tina gazed up to see the van's rear hatch hanging open. A few more heads of broccoli rolled out, bouncing off NoWay's hood.

The hover-van touched down beside them. Its back end was crumpled.

Jennica winced. "Then if it's illegal, that makes those guys . . ."

An angry face glared through the van's passenger window.

"Broccoli smugglers!" cried NoWay and Clorox together.

Two Rhunnin men and a Pockadoo woman piled out of the vehicle. Judging by their scowls, they were not card-carrying members of the Earth Kids Fan Club.

The crooked-horned Pockadoo snarled. Her Rhunnin companions planted their fists on their hips, glaring from their spilled cargo to the crew in the hovercraft. One had a scarred face, like he'd been in a knife fight.

"We're all going to die," said Booker calmly.

"Um, do you think we should . . . ," Mateo began.

"Go!" cried Tina. "Go, now!"

As the three smugglers stalked toward the hovercraft with vicious intent, NoWay fumbled at the vehicle's controls. Leaning past him, Clorox punched a button and hauled back the joystick. The craft's roof slid closed. *"Sheeglockitta!"* she cried.

Mateo assumed that meant *Floor it!* because that's exactly what NoWay did. The smugglers' outstretched hands slipped off the hover-car as it rocketed up from the ground, narrowly missing a passing hover-bus.

Glancing back, Booker reported, "They're climbing back into their van. Aaand . . . yup, they're chasing us. We're all going to die."

"Stop saying that," said Jennica. "We can't die."

"Why not?" asked Booker.

"If we die, I'll never get another babysitting job again."

Tina cocked her head. "You say that like it's a bad thing."

The Earth kids were jostled from side to side as

NoWay whipped around corners, trying to evade the smugglers. The van driver stuck on their tail.

NoWay cut behind a line of trees. The van followed. He zigzagged among office buildings. Again, the van followed.

"Yup, they're gonna catch us and eat our livers," said Booker, as calmly as if he was reporting the weather.

"Not if I can help it," growled Tina.

"No, we find Elvis, hurry back to the portal, and get home before your parents do," said Jennica. "I made them a promise, and I intend to keep it."

They zipped around another corner and suddenly a pedestrian crossing loomed right before them.

"Bridge!" cried the Earth kids.

NoWay dove, but too late.

"Aaaagh!"

The bottom edge of the bridge caught the roof of their car. Everyone ducked.

SCREEEEEEEE-GRUNK!

The roof hatch detached and went sailing behind them.

Glancing back, Mateo watched the broad sheet of metal fly right into the van's windshield. Blinded, the driver plowed his vehicle into the bridge.

KRONCH!

And that was all he could see as NoWay zoomed off, fleeing the accident scene. After a few more high-speed twists and turns, NoWay slowed, checking over his shoulder.

"Did we lose them?" he asked.

Twisting around to check out the back window, Jennica said, "No sign of smugglers."

"For now," said Booker darkly.

"Now is what matters," said Mateo. "NoWay, can you get us to that science lab?"

NoWay flashed a thumbs-up, then focused on the road ahead of them. As they cruised past some bottle-shaped buildings that might have been offices, he muttered, "I'm sure I'll spot something familiar soon . . ."

Clorox sighed. "Slow down."

"I can find it." NoWay squinted at the buildings like they were a full sheet of unanswered math problems.

Leaning out, Clorox waved and shouted to a pedestrian just below them. She asked a question in the alien language. All Mateo caught was the word *Kwako*.

The man below responded with a flurry of words and wiggly gestures. He was either giving them directions or inventing a brand-new dance. Clorox thanked him.

"Aw, you didn't need to ask directions," said NoWay. "I would've found it."

"Sometime this year?" murmured Booker. Mateo stifled a smile.

Up one avenue and down another they went, weaving through Boogbee's sprawl. At last, the hovercraft reached a series of interlocking domes.

"See?" said NoWay. "I would absolutely have found it."

Jennica and Clorox shared an amused glance. "Nice to know that boys are just as clueless on Kroon," said Jennica.

"Hey!" said all the boys. The girls just smiled.

After parking the vehicle beside a row of other hover-cars and -vans, NoWay climbed out and assessed the damage. That walkway had torn the roof away, like it had been lopped off by Kroon's biggest bagel slicer. NoWay hid his face in his hands.

Jennica patted the boy's shoulder. "Just tell your parents that you always wanted a convertible."

NoWay shook his head. Through his hands, he moaned something that sounded like, "I am so dead."

Taking NoWay's elbow, Clorox steered him toward the building entrance. Just then, a Klaxon blared, emitting a series of rising tones: *Toom toom toom!*

"Hold on to something!" cried Clorox.

Tina gripped Mateo's hand.

"Something hefty!" yelled NoWay.

"Why, is it the heavy gravity again?" asked Jennica, strolling toward a nearby tree.

The alien teens grabbed on to a parked hovercraft. "No!" cried Clorox. "Versa-visa!"

At that exact instant, Mateo felt that feeling you get just before the roller coaster drops: momentary weightlessness. But this time it wasn't momentary.

It was like someone had turned off the gravity.

With nothing pressing down on him, Mateo's feet left the ground.

"Whoa!"

Desperate, he threw himself toward a railing that bordered the walkway. His hands fumbled at the cool metal and finally caught, just as his legs lifted above his head. Tina screamed, rising past him into the air.

"Grab my legs!" cried Mateo.

In a frantic lunge, Tina managed to grip his ankle before she floated into the sky. Jennica was hugging a tree. But Booker hadn't been so lucky.

"Help!" he yelled, drifting up past Tina.

She waved her leg. "Hold my foot!"

Breast-stroking his way through the air, Booker barely managed to catch Tina's shoelaces. For a few breaths, they hung like that, in an upside-down chain. Then . . .

"You're untying my shoe," said Tina.

"I can't help it." Booker stretched out his other hand, trying to grab her foot. He couldn't quite reach. And he couldn't tug on the shoelaces to bring himself closer, for fear of popping her shoe off.

"Curl your toes back," he said.

"Grab my foot," Tina said.

"I'm trying."

Mateo looked up, past his own body and past Tina's. Bit by bit, Booker's grip was steadily untying the bow that held her sneaker on. Another few seconds, and their friend would drift into space holding a pink sneaker.

"Hang on, Book!" cried Mateo.

"You know," said Booker, "now that I'm faced with death, I find I'm not so keen on dying."

Mateo winced. "You're not going to die."

The slipknot in Tina's shoe was nearly undone. One more inch to go.

"M-make sure my little brother doesn't get my Star Wars a-action figures," Booker choked out. "He'll only wreck them."

Then, with a tiny pop, the knot untied, and the shoe slipped off.

Booker was in deep, deep doo-doo.

Chapter 10
BLINDED WITH SCIENCE

ooker's eyes went huge with terror.

He floated upward, still holding Tina's sneaker by its lace.

"Booker, no!" cried Mateo. His heart plummeted.

Was this the end of his best friend? Mateo could kick himself for getting Booker into this situation. But of course, if he kicked, he'd lose Tina, too.

And then, with a *toom toom toom*, the Klaxon sounded again, this time in descending tones. For a long beat, nothing happened.

Gradually, Mateo felt his body drift back downward, legs returning to the ground with Tina attached. As soon as he was right side up, he craned his neck, searching for Booker.

Slowly, slowly, as if descending on an escalator like a pageant princess, Booker floated down out of the lavender sky. He gave a little finger wave and a weak smile.

Mateo turned to the aliens. "That's outrageous!" he said. "How can you live like this?"

Clorox and NoWay shrugged. "You get used to it," said the boy.

"Now, shall we go?" said Clorox. "Let us see if scientists have your dog."

Shaken, Booker landed, hunched over with his hands on his knees. He held up a pointer finger. "First, promise me something."

"What's that?" asked NoWay.

"Next chance we get, let's buy me some concrete booties."

The Earth kids' laughter had a nervous edge to it. The Rhunnin teens looked puzzled.

Trailing NoWay and Clorox, the Earthlings bounded up to the main dome's entrance. A door slid open as they approached.

Inside, aliens dressed in baby blue jumpsuits hurried about, acting important. Most were Rhunnin, but Jennica spotted a few Pockadoos and Naugas among them. Diversity hiring practices. Jennica approved.

Clorox made her way over to an official-looking desk staffed by an official-looking Nauga. The woman scowled at her. Mateo was beginning to think this was a Nauga's default expression. While Clorox consulted with the woman, NoWay drew the Earth kids aside.

"We must be very careful in here," he said.

"Why?" Tina glowered. "If these guys have our dog, *they're* the ones who should be careful."

"This lab is, how do you say, retracted?"

"Restricted?" Jennica suggested.

NoWay nodded. "Yes. Restricted. Security is tighter than a nurlock's fimbong." He paused as if waiting for a response to a joke.

"So . . . that's tight?" asked Mateo.

"The tightest," NoWay agreed. "Clorox is telling them you are Earth scientists who want to observe their monster experiments."

Booker scratched his cheek. "Think it'll work?"

"We'll see," said the alien boy.

Jennica touched NoWay's arm. "Thanks for doing this," she said. "We couldn't have gotten this far without you."

He beamed at her and took her hand. "I am happy to help. It has been my dream to meet Earth people and one day visit Earth."

Just then, Clorox joined them. She narrowed her eyes at how chummy NoWay and Jennica were getting. But all she said was, "They're ready for us."

The crew followed her over to the desk, where the Nauga woman handed them each a silver dollar–size disk on a cord. With gestures, she indicated they should hang it around their necks and insert the disks in their ears.

"But it won't fit," said Booker.

NoWay grinned. "It's a LingoPop. Another of Grunthar's brilliant inventions."

"It shapes to ear," said Clorox. "Then you can talk in any language—even ours."

"This would've really helped in French class," Jennica muttered.

After everyone had inserted the disks, NoWay said, "See? Now I'm talking to you in Rhunninish, and it sounds like your language."

"Cool," said Mateo. "Now can we go see the labs?"

Just then, a Pockadoo approached. "Follow me," he said in a voice deeper than Darth Vader's. "Honored Earth guests, my name is Woolfie."

They trailed him over to a panel, where he pressed his enormous palm to the wall and tapped a rhythm with his fingertips. The panel slid aside with a whoosh. It revealed a long, tubular corridor lined with observation windows that looked in on a series of rooms.

"Our experiments take place in this section," boomed Woolfie, waving a hand at the windows.

"Where are the, uh, monsters?" asked Mateo.

The orange man pointed farther down the hall. As the group followed him, Mateo peered into the rooms they passed. In one, a scientist wearing a freaky-looking helmet pounded his head with what looked like a rubber fish. In another, three scientists were tickling a giant worm.

Of course, he thought. *Just ordinary science stuff.*

Soon they stopped before a room where the experimenters were shining different colored lights onto a half dozen hairy creatures that resembled fat cats with butterfly wings. The Pockadoo gestured. "Here, we are studying whether color will affect the fizzbo's milk production."

"Mmm." NoWay nodded as if he were thinking deeply about the experiment. "And has it?"

"Not yet," said Woolfie.

"What's the weirdest monster here?" asked Tina, trying to hurry them along to find Elvis.

The Pockadoo scientist rubbed one of his horns. "Possibly the chooka-chooka-wee in the next room." He led them along the corridor. "It only eats once a year. We're trying to learn how such a big monster survives on so little."

The next chamber was larger than the rest. And it was nearly filled by a vast blue-and-yellow-mottled creature with a forest of what looked like electrodes attached to its bulk. Two scientists crammed into one corner took readings from their handheld devices.

"This is all fascinating," said Mateo. "But we're wondering whether you have any Earth monsters here?"

Woolfie stuck out his tongue and made a noise like someone choking on a chicken bone. "Earth monsters? Ha! Much easier to get Earth pizza than Earth monsters." He leaned closer. "Speaking of Earth pizza—"

"No, we didn't bring any," said Tina.

"I was planning to ask if you prefer thin crust or thick?" said the Pockadoo.

"Thin," said Jennica.

"Thick," said Booker.

"All pizza is good pizza," said Mateo.

Tina scowled, shifting from foot to foot. "Can we move on? Please?"

A flurry of activity in the room across the hall caught Mateo's attention. "What's happening there?" he asked.

The group shuffled over to the window.

"Ah," said Woolfie. "Our TransMog Ray experiments."

NoWay raised a triumphant finger. "Another Grunthar invention!"

"Yeah, we get it," said Booker. "The dude invented everything from snuggly socks to sliced bread."

NoWay's eyebrows rose. "You mean you Earth persons *slice* your bread?"

Booker waved him off.

As the Earth kids watched, a Nauga scientist aimed a football-shaped ray gun at a scaly monster that was a cross between an iguana and a beaver. The thing shuddered. Its outline seemed to blur, and two blinks later, it was a horse-size creature with six legs.

"Whoa!" said Mateo.

"And giddyap," said Booker.

"The ray transmogrifies the monsters into a different form," said Woolfie. "We're studying how their behavior changes when their form does."

"Does it change?" asked Clorox.

Woolfie lifted an enormous shoulder. "Not so far. But we keep experimenting."

With a worried look, Jennica said, "Poor things. Is the change permanent?"

"No, it wears off in—"

"Just two hours!" said NoWay. "So cool."

A crafty look crossed Booker's face. "Does that thing work on people, too?"

"Of course," said the Pockadoo.

With a chuckle, Booker told Mateo, "Imagine turning Principal Zakowski into a skunk."

Woolfie frowned. "But we would never experiment on people."

"No, of course not," said Booker. "Still . . ."

Tina, feeling antsy, strode off on her own to check the other rooms for signs of Elvis. But something about the TransMog Ray tickled something at the back of Mateo's mind.

"Can we go in there?" he asked.

The Pockadoo glanced from him to the scientist.

He tapped on the glass to catch the Nauga's attention, then gestured from his guests to the room. The Nauga nodded.

After flipping open a control panel on the wall by the window, Woolfie laid his palm on it. A door-shaped section of the wall slid up, and the Pockadoo led the crew down a ramp and into the lab.

Ignoring them, the Nauga scientist continued testing the monster with several devices.

"That thing's not going to eat us, is it?" asked Booker.

"It's a vegetarian," said Woolfie.

"Sure." Booker made a face. "That's what it wants you to think."

Spotting a doorway at the back of the lab, Mateo asked, "What's back there?"

"The monsters' permanent cages," said the Pockadoo. He checked a handheld computer. "I can show you, but then you must go. I have work to do."

Behind the door stretched a narrow corridor between two rows of glassed-in cages. About a dozen monsters of all shapes and sizes inhabited them. Some paced, some slept, some flitted about. Mateo's eye was drawn to a big beetle-bunny hybrid.

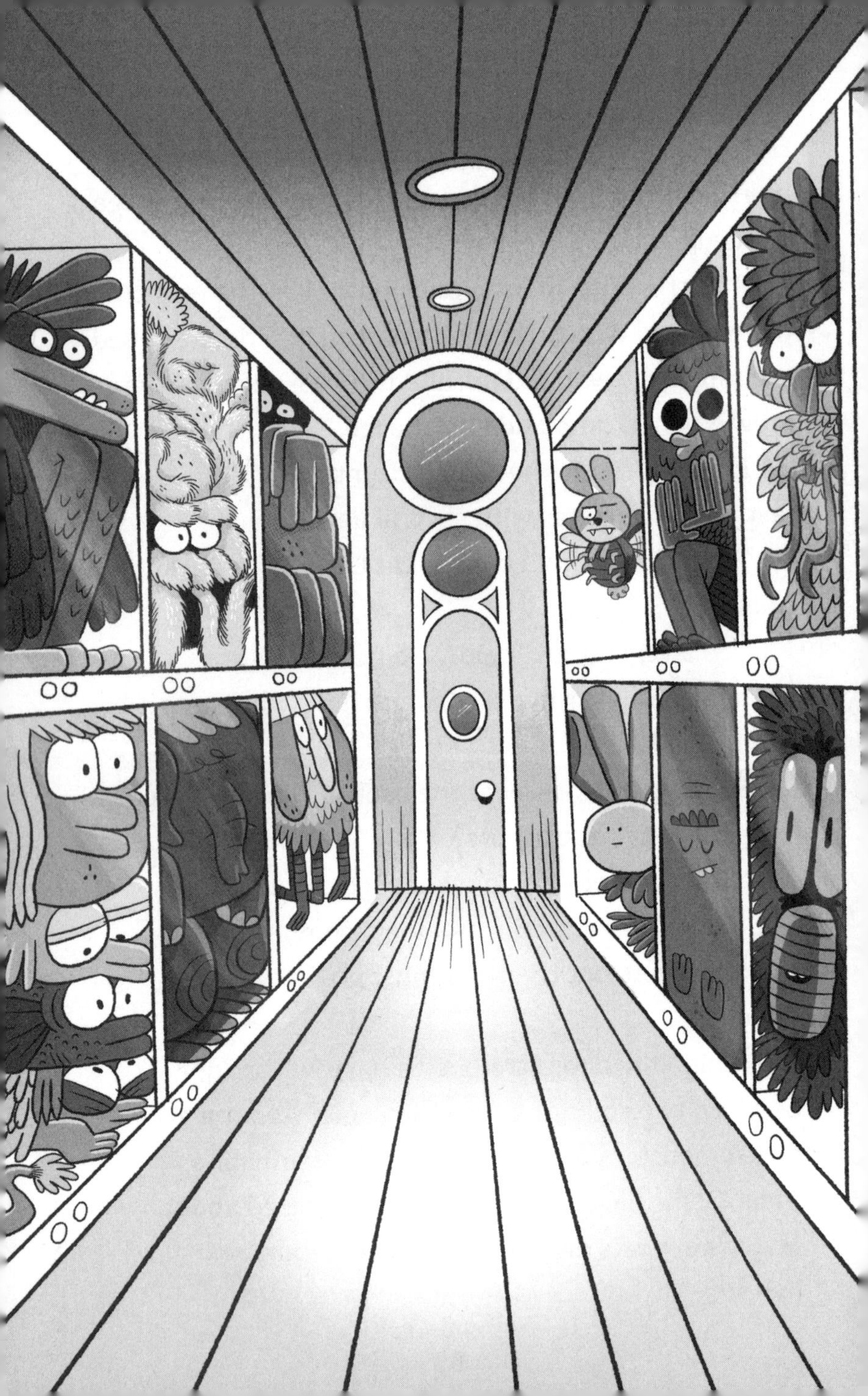

"Hey, that's a foofaloofa, like at Grunthar's," he said, approaching the cage. Mateo tapped on the glass. "Hi, buddy!"

The foofaloofa glanced up at the noise.

"Come say hello," said Mateo.

At this, the foofaloofa's eyes narrowed, its antennae bristled, and then, without warning, it scuttled straight toward Mateo, snapping its sharp front teeth.

Chapter 11
SAVAGE BUNNY

Bam! **The monster** slammed up against the glass. Mateo had never been frightened by a rabbit before, but there's a first time for everything. The foofaloofa's wild eyes were red-rimmed. Its antennae aimed like spears. Despite the glass barrier, the creature chomped its teeth at him over and over, trying to get out.

"Yikes!" Mateo scooted back, heartbeat racing.

Woolfie frowned. "Don't annoy the monsters. Some are quite dangerous." Spreading his arms wide, he herded the group back out of the corridor and through the lab. "Time to go now."

When they reentered the observation corridor, Tina was waiting.

"Any luck?" Mateo asked.

"Nothing." She clenched her fists. "Ugh, I'm so sick of this. Every lead we get on Elvis turns out to be a dead end."

A corner of Booker's mouth turned up. "Just like in *The Mystery Club*."

"Huh?" said Tina.

Mateo nodded, getting it. "Every episode, they have to follow a bunch of red herrings before they finally solve the mystery."

"What do fish have to do with anything?" asked NoWay. "Are they mysterious?"

"It's— Oh, never mind," said Mateo.

The Pockadoo scientist returned them to the entry hall and reclaimed their LingoPops. He strode off without even a goodbye.

"It's late," said Jennica, leading the group back to their hovercraft. "We don't know how quickly time passes here, and I need to get you back home before your parents return. We should leave now."

"*No!*" chorused Tina and Mateo.

"One more try?" Mateo begged. "Please?"

Tina clenched her jaw. "You have to let us visit that politician. It's our last chance to find Elvis."

"We can't just leave him here," said Mateo.

For a long moment, she stared at the two of them. Then, with a sigh, Jennica agreed.

The government offices rested in rolling parkland

a short distance outside Boogbee City. Mateo assumed this was so that the residents didn't have to witness the ugliness that is government in action. (He'd once done a project about the state legislature.)

As they flew along, Booker noticed the sky darkening from lavender to an ugly bruised shade of purple. Heavy blue clouds rolled in from the horizon.

"Uh, do you guys have hurricanes or tornadoes here?" asked Booker.

"No, why?" said Clorox.

"Because it looks like something bad is about to happen."

Tina shook her head. "You're always such an optimist."

"No, he's correct." Staring out at the clouds, NoWay bit his lip. "Clorox, we should . . ."

"Right away," she agreed, pushing the joystick forward and descending.

"What is it?" asked Jennica. "What's happening?"

A few thick yellow-green spatters hit the seats and windshield.

"That looks like snot," said Mateo. "Why is it raining snot?"

Clorox dove more sharply as the spattering increased. "It's a goo storm," she said, angling the vehicle toward a stand of trees beside a small hill. "We can't travel in it."

More goo rained down on them. Without its roof, the hovercraft was going to turn into a flying snot bucket if this kept up.

"Maybe not the best time to drive a convertible," said Mateo.

The vehicle landed with a bump. "Quick, get under those trees," said Clorox.

Wiping the goo from his arms, Booker asked, "This stuff won't eat away our skin, will it? Or turn us into mutant toad people?"

"Let's not find out." Jennica hustled away from the hover-car and beelined it for the shelter of the trees.

The others joined her. Squeezing together, the friends hugged the tree trunks for protection. But as the goo storm worsened, it blasted through the leaves as if they weren't there.

"We need—*ack!*—better shelter," said Mateo, spitting out the goo that had splashed into his mouth. It tasted like brussels sprouts and rancid cheese. Not exactly Baskin-Robbins's flavor of the month.

Shading her eyes from the spatters, Jennica scanned their surroundings. Her gaze landed on the little hill. "Look! Is that a cave?"

"I don't care if it's someone's back pocket," said Booker. "I just don't want to drown in snot."

"Let's go!" cried NoWay.

He dashed toward the hillock and its cave. Everyone piled into the opening after him. Despite the driving goo storm, Mateo paused, squinting at the blue-and-yellow vegetation covering the little hill. It looked somehow familiar. But this was no time to figure out why. He dove into the cave last of all.

Inside, it was warm and gamey smelling, but free of goo. Everyone crowded together in the tight space. Rather than a rock floor, the cave bottom was kind of spongy, like moss.

"Ewwww." Jennica shuddered. She tried in vain to wipe off the slime that covered her. "That's so gross."

"How do you live like this?" asked Tina. When Clorox started to respond, she held up a palm. "I know, I know: You get used to it."

"Mostly," said NoWay.

Jennica held up her phone light to illuminate the space. The cave formed a near-perfect arch, tall enough for them to hunch over but not fully stand. Toward the back, it sloped down so low you'd have to belly-crawl under the tear-shaped blob dangling from the ceiling, before finally disappearing into darkness.

"This place stinks," said Tina. "How long do we have to stay here?"

Mateo peeked out the entrance. "It's still goo-ing out there." It seemed to him that the cave opening was slightly lower than when they'd entered. He rubbed his eyes. Was he imagining things?

"Is the cave . . . closing?" asked Booker.

"Impossible," said Clorox.

Mateo squinted into the growing dimness. "No, he's right."

"Let's get out of here." Booker pushed his way forward.

"But the goo storm . . . ," said NoWay.

Mateo joined Booker. "Forget the goo. We've gotta—"

But just before they reached the entrance, it shut with a snap. Darkness fell.

"What the—?" Jennica gasped. Using all their might, Booker and Mateo pounded and pushed at the wall with fists and feet. Nothing budged. They were sealed in good and tight.

The faint light of Jennica's cell phone revealed their predicament. No other exits—except the one at the back of the cave. And Mateo had a bad feeling about that one.

"We're trapped," he said.

"You know," said Booker, "I'm starting to think this isn't really a cave."

"Oh yeah?" said Tina. "What clued you in?"

And then Mateo recalled where he'd seen the hill's blue-and-yellow vegetation before. Icy dread plunged into the pit of his stomach.

"Uh, guys," he said. "I just figured out where we are."

"Where?" asked Tina.

Despite his fear, Mateo's voice stayed calm. "Remember that huge monster we saw in the lab? The one that only eats once a year?"

"The chooka-chooka-wee?" said Clorox.

"I think we're inside one's . . . mouth."

In the cell phone's dim light, everyone looked spooked.

"And you know what that makes us?" Mateo asked.

Booker's mouth formed a grim line. But all he said was "Lunch."

Chapter 12

ROBOT GUIDE

On the plus side, the chooka-chooka-wee didn't seem to have any teeth to grind them up with. On the minus side, its mouth-cave was getting . . . mighty moist. Something dripped from the roof, and a gooey tide was slowly rising around their shoes.

"Gross!" said Jennica. "Are we being digested?"

"The good news is," said NoWay, "this thing only eats once a year."

Tina glared. "How is that good? We're its annual meal!"

"I think he means digestion is slow," said Clorox. "We have time to plan."

Mateo's chest felt tight, and his mouth was dryer than a summer in the Sahara. When he glanced over, Booker was staring at nothing, muttering to himself. Mateo touched his friend's shoulder.

"Book, I'm so sorry I got you into this," he said. "You don't deserve . . ."

Booker's smile was wobbly. "Hey, I said friends stick together. I just didn't think we'd be digested together, too."

Drawing a shaky breath, Mateo wiped his palms on his jeans. This was it. If he wanted to be a hero, now was the time. Mateo tried to think logically, like the kids on *Mystery Club*. But the only logical thought his helpful mind repeated was *We're all gonna die, we're all gonna die, we're all gonna die!*

He took another deep breath, blew it out, and said the first thing that came to mind. "What are our resources?"

"Huh?" said Booker.

"What do we have with us that could help?"

Everyone dug into their pockets. They produced: a pencil stub, a key fob, two stale cookies, cell phones, spare change, a debit card, some string, and from NoWay's pocket . . .

"What's that?" asked Jennica.

The cell phone light revealed NoWay's blush. "It's . . . mmm . . . a mama toe?"

Mateo frowned. "It doesn't look like a toe."

Resting on NoWay's palm, the disk looked more like a pink hockey puck.

"Where did you get that?" asked Clorox.

NoWay's blush deepened, and his shoulders climbed in an awkward shrug. "I borrowed it?"

"From where?"

In a tiny voice, NoWay said, "Grunthar's home."

"What?!" said Clorox.

"I wanted something to remember our visit by."

"A *memento*?" said Mateo.

NoWay pointed at him. "That's the word."

Bringing her cell phone light closer, Jennica asked, "Yeah, but what is it? What's it do?"

"Well, it . . ." NoWay turned the puck this way and that. "I don't know."

Tina planted her hands on her hips. "Come on! Is it an invention or a paperweight?"

Mateo plucked the disk from NoWay's grasp and turned it this way and that. He pinched it, prodded it, shook it, and smelled it. "It's a real hockey puck," he said.

"Well, that's super helpful against a monster," Booker growled.

Mateo had to agree.

But then his gaze wandered to the back of the cave, to the massive uvula hanging there, and a thought struck him. A truly un-Mateo thought. *What would happen if I tossed this into the monster's gullet?*

Before he could second-guess himself, Mateo bent and side-armed the puck into the dangly thing at the back of the chooka-chooka-wee's mouth.

"My mama toe!" cried NoWay.

For a handful of heartbeats, nothing happened. Juices dripped from the roof, the mouth stayed shut, and everyone held their breath.

Then Booker sighed. His shoulders slumped.

"Nice try," he said. "Anyone got any other ideas?"

By the fading light of Jennica's phone, Mateo could make out everyone's disappointed expressions. He silently cursed himself. *That'll teach you to act without thinking. Now what?*

Something rumbled at the back of the mouth cave.

"Is it growling?" said Tina.

"Or digesting?" said Booker.

The rumble intensified, rising in pitch.

"Whatever it's doing, it's—" Mateo began.

And then, a foul-smelling tide erupted from the back of the mouth. It was the paragon of puke, the ultimate in upchuck, and it blasted out with the force of a firehose.

Someone screamed. "Ahh! We're gonna drown!"

But before that could happen, the mouth cave flew open. Everyone shot out like cannon balls, swept away on a wave of monster barf.

BLAARRRRGH!

WHUMP!

They sprawled onto the blue grass, thoroughly drenched, and smelling like a ripe dumpster in the summer sun. Everyone scrambled farther away. After all, who knew whether the monster had a long tongue?

"Ewww-yuck!" said Clorox, shaking chooka-chooka-wee puke from her arms.

"Just *yuck*," said Jennica. "Or *ewww*. Both are appropriate."

Booker pinched his nose. "Man, we reek."

"A hundred showers won't be enough," Mateo agreed.

Tina patted his shoulder. "But hey, at least we're not dead. Nice move, bro."

Mateo smiled at this rare compliment from his sister.

"Now let's hustle," she said, clapping her hands together. "Time is short."

"And we've got a dog to rescue!" Mateo cried.

Fortunately, the goo storm had petered out while they were inside the mouth cave. After scooping handfuls of slime out of the convertible hovercraft, the soggy crew headed off to the government office complex. In short order, they reached a sprawling collection of mismatched buildings. Some were domes, several were mushroom-shaped, and one looked like an enormous PlayStation controller.

"Huh," said Mateo. "That looks just like . . ."

"Our architects were inspired by some Earth objects," said NoWay. "Design is very—how to say?—slicing edge?"

"Cutting edge?" said Jennica. "I'll say."

The parking area was chock-full of sleek hovercraft that made NoWay's battered ride look like the last kid picked for pickleball. Following a winding path, the gang approached the buildings.

NoWay stopped to consult a site map on a nearby pedestal. He pointed to one of the giant mushrooms. "Pennzoil's over there."

"We do not exactly look fashionable," said Clorox, surveying the gooey bunch. Their clothes were stained and damp, and their hair looked like someone had gone nutso with the styling gel. "I would love to change clothes."

"Seriously?" Tina crossed her arms. "This isn't a beauty contest, it's a rescue."

"She's right," said Jennica. "If we're going to get us home in time, we can't stop for a costume change."

Clorox sighed. "No one cares about fashion anymore."

Down the path NoWay guided them, hurrying over to the mushroom-shaped building. Inside its circular entryway, a Rhunnin woman with high green hair perched in a wheeled seat behind three desks arranged in a semicircle.

Clorox approached her, asking, "Pennzoil?"

Green Hair pointed to the desk on the left, and the girl walked around to stand in front of it. After looking the crew up and down, the receptionist motored over on her chair to help Clorox.

"How come she wouldn't help us from the center desk?" Tina asked NoWay.

"Impossible," said NoWay. "Different desks for different offices."

Booker scratched his cheek. "You guys have some interesting rules."

"You have no idea," said NoWay.

Clorox chatted with the receptionist, indicating the Earth kids behind her. The woman's expression brightened.

"No pizza," said Booker.

Green Hair's face fell.

"But if you let us in, we'll send you some," said Mateo. As if he had any idea how to do that.

Still, the promise seemed good enough for Green Hair. The receptionist handed them each a brown square about half the size of a chocolate bar and tapped her own chest. "Put on," she said.

They complied. Mateo noticed his brown square didn't stick to his shirt but hovered a half inch away, as if the shirt's gravity held it in place. Pretty fancy name tag.

When everyone was ready, Green Hair pressed a button on her console, and a two-foot-high robot motored out from what looked like a broom closet. The robot looked a bit like a vacuum canister with a square head and four pointy arm extensions. It scanned each of the visitors with a green laser that beamed from its chest, then spoke a few words in an alien language. Clorox responded.

The robot then addressed the Earth kids in English.

"Hello, jolly visitors Earthling-type!" it said. "My pleasure is to welcoming you!"

NoWay nudged Jennica. "It speaks six hundred languages."

"You mean five hundred and ninety-nine?" she said, wincing at the machine's mangled grammar.

"Be following me jolly well please," the robot announced. Swiveling its head around, it rolled over to a wall panel. The robot inserted an arm into a slot, the panel slid aside, and they all entered a tiny room. The panel slid shut. A faint hum sounded.

"Is this an elevator?" asked Jennica.

"Or a death trap?" said Booker.

Mateo shrugged. "Either way, I'm glad they don't have elevator music."

"Music?" said the robot. A second later, it emitted a cheesy melody that sounded like ABBA's "Dancing Queen" being played on a garbage disposal. "Jolly, jolly music."

Mateo blew out a sigh.

Nobody could tell whether the elevator was going up, sideways, or standing still, so smoothly did it move. But twenty seconds later, the door slid open. "Hey, hey, hey," said the robot. "All the way!"

When it rolled out into a golden hallway, everyone

followed. At the far end, the robot motored up to a wall panel and inserted a spindly arm. With a *shhhoook*, the panel slid back to reveal an office.

At least Mateo thought it was an office. The floor practically vibrated in electric lime green. Video monitors covered two walls. A shallow pool zigzagged through the room. And behind a purple horseshoe of a desk sat a round little Rhunnin man with his back to them.

First in the alien tongue, then in English, the robot said, "Most jolly you are to be meeting boss man. Introduction: Pennzoil the Most Groovy and Smart-Smart Fellow, Head Gnorft for District Three!"

At this, the round little man swiveled to face them, looked up, and said, "Howdy, y'all."

Chapter 13

JUMPING THROUGH HOOPS

Mateo's first thought was that people must regularly confuse Pennzoil with Humpty Dumpty. The egg-shaped man had no neck to speak of. His head blended right into his body. He wore a tall hat with two peaks, a wine-colored robe, and a smile so wide it practically wrapped around his head.

"How marvelous!" crowed Pennzoil, coming around the desk to meet them. "How historic! Our first Earth visitors."

"Um, greetings from our planet," said Jennica.

Pennzoil held up his hand with the palm facing her. After a moment's hesitation, she gave him a high five. Judging from the look on his face, he'd been expecting something less slappy. But he quickly recovered.

"This is an honor," he said. "Your planet's historical broadcasts are truly popular on Kroon. I personally enjoy histories of your American West. Howdy, pardner! Yee-haw." His cowboy impression sounded more like a cheesy radio deejay, but the Earth kids forced a smile.

"Mr. Pennzoil, we need your help," said Mateo.

"Our dog came through the portal, and we can't find him," said Tina.

Folding his arms, Pennzoil leaned back against his desk. "Tell me more."

The crew took turns relating their adventures on Kroon—the near miss with the chooka-chooka-wee, Monster Control, the private zoo, Grunthar, even their run-in with the smugglers.

Pennzoil's eyes widened. "Broccoli smugglers?" He stroked his nose. "The lowest scum. I will deal with them."

"We really need your help finding Elvis, and—" Jennica began.

Tina cut in. "Do you have our dog? Yes or no?"

Pennzoil blinked at the interruption. "Why, no."

"Tina, don't be rude," said Jennica. "We're asking a favor."

Tina scowled, jamming her hands into her pockets.

Mateo felt close to despair. *Another* dead end? It was dawning on him that they might never find his sweet knuckleheaded dog. That they would never play fetch together or go for another walk. A lump rose in his throat. He turned away.

"We have to leave, like, now," Jennica told Pennzoil. "We're desperate. Is there anything you can do?"

"Of course, of course," said the politician. "A dog is higher life form. I will be happy to use the powers of my office to help you."

Mateo and Tina exchanged a hopeful look.

"But first you must fill out some forms."

Booker frowned. *"Forms?"*

"But we're out of time," said the babysitter.

"It won't take long," said Pennzoil. "It's just, for any government actions, the proper forms must be completed. Understand?"

"I guess," said Mateo.

Rubbing his hands together, Pennzoil reached across the desk and picked up an oval-shaped computer tablet. He passed it to Clorox. "Your friend here can translate for you. While you work, I will send messages to my contacts. We will find your dog."

You'd better, thought Mateo. But he didn't say it.

Taking a seat on a wide purple bench, the crew went to work. NoWay peered over Clorox's shoulder at the first form.

"Let's see," he said. "First question: What district are you from?"

"Um, Pomona?" said Jennica.

Clorox nodded. "I'll put 'Earth.' Next, how many fremblewimps in your family?"

Tina shot Mateo a questioning look. He shrugged. "None?"

And so it went. Over half of the questions made no sense, so they were able to complete the form quickly.

"All done," Clorox said, handing the tablet back to Pennzoil.

He paused in his texting, or whatever he was up to on his wrist-mounted computer. "Groovy. I will pull up the next one."

"*Next* one?" Jennica echoed. "We've got to go."

Pennzoil's frown was sorrowful. "I'm sorry, I thought you wanted to locate your dog?"

"We do!" said Mateo and Tina together.

"Then please continue. By law, I cannot help unless you complete the proper forms." Pennzoil tapped away on the tablet and passed it to Clorox.

So they filled out a second form.

And a third.

And a fourth.

By the sixth form, Tina was long past impatient and rounding on ticked off. "Enough!" she cried. "Look, we don't even live here. No way we should have to fill out so many stupid forms."

"You shouldn't," said NoWay.

Pennzoil looked up from his wrist computer. "You're right, Earth girl. No more forms."

Tina and Mateo relaxed. "Great," he said. "Now—"

"But you must complete the agility test before I can help you," said Pennzoil. "Very important."

Booker scowled. "Agility test? Give me a break."

"What would you like broken?" asked Pennzoil.

"He means this is ridiculous," said Mateo.

Tina muttered, "I'd like to break something."

Pennzoil lifted a shoulder. "The law is the law."

The politician hopped up from his chair and then led them over to the wall without video screens. It slid back to reveal a second, much larger room. Inside, they saw a set of rings hanging from a horizontal pole, two lines of cones stretching the length of the room, a pair of stilts, and a series of hoops.

"Seriously?" said Mateo.

"Is this a government office or gymnastics class?" said Tina.

Jennica tapped her foot. "This is taking forever."

Pennzoil smiled apologetically. "I'm sorry, buckaroos, but my hands are hog-tied. Rules are rules."

"This is a joke, right?" Booker asked the alien teens. Clorox and NoWay shook their heads.

"Everyone must complete the circuit," said the politician.

"And that's *all*?" said Mateo.

"That's all," said Pennzoil.

"Nothing more?" asked Mateo. "You'll help us then?"

The egg-shaped man leaned against the wall and said, "You may begin."

One after the other, Mateo and the rest swung on the rings, dodged between the cones, and jumped through the hoops. When they finished, everyone was sweaty and red-faced. Pennzoil took notes on his computer. Or maybe he was playing an alien video game. It was hard to tell.

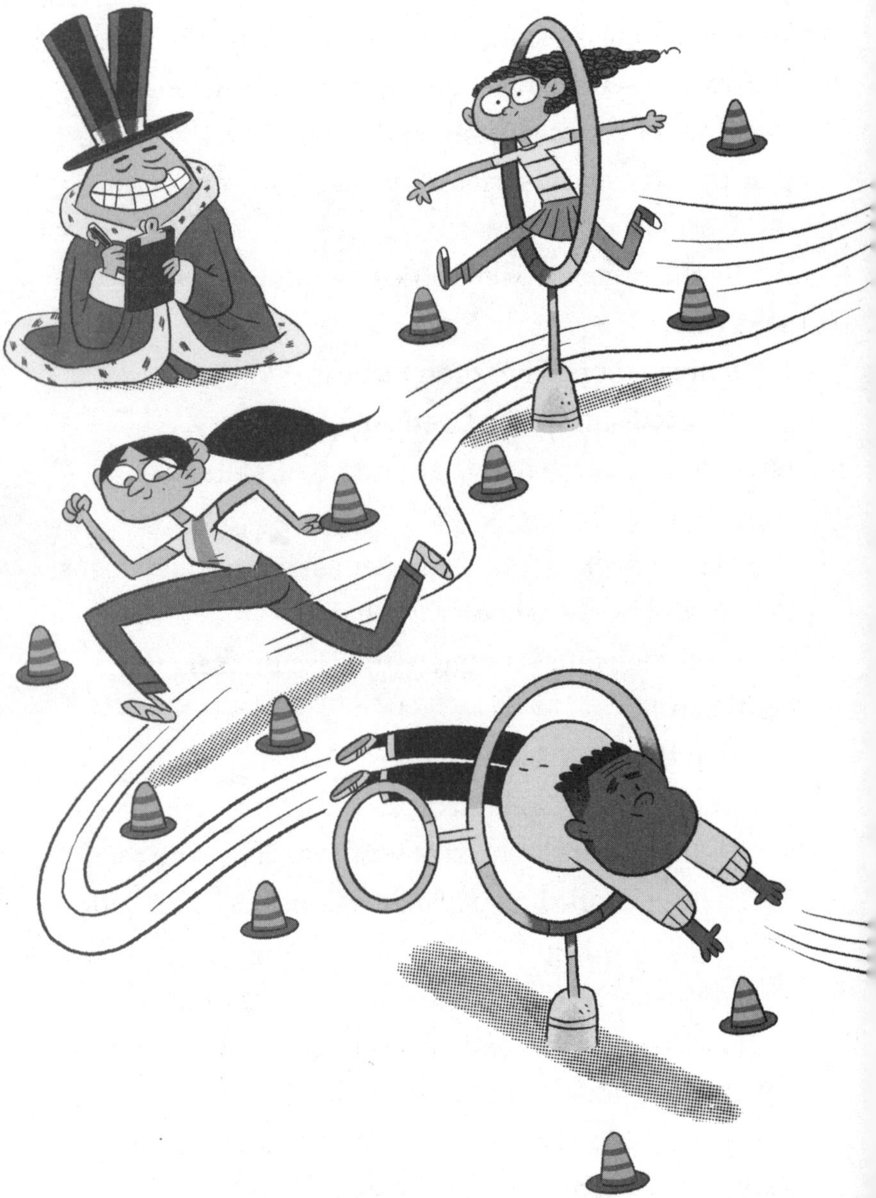

"Okay, mister," said Tina. "We did what you asked. Where's Elvis?"

Pennzoil beamed at them like they'd just won the jillion-dollar sweepstakes. "Certainly, certainly. Come right this way!"

He led them over to the wall panel. It slid back to reveal Pennzoil's office, which was now filled with three angry broccoli smugglers. The crooked-horned Pockadoo snarled. The Rhunnins pounded their fists into their palms.

"Remember when I said we were dead before?" asked Booker.

"Yeah?" said Mateo.

"This time we're *really, really* dead."

And for once, Mateo couldn't disagree.

Chapter 14

NEVER MESS WITH A GYMNAST

With a wild cry, the three smugglers rushed forward. The Earth kids and their alien friends scattered.

The Rhunnin with a nasty scar on his face ran at Tina with arms spread wide. She did a back handspring, leaped for the rings, and swung both feet up, directly into the alien's gut.

Whump! Down went Scarface like a sack of beans.

"Never mess with a gymnast," said Tina.

Crooked Horns made a grab for Clorox. Ducking under the Pockadoo's arm, she ran a zigzag pattern through the cones. Oddly enough, the smuggler followed her path, tripped over her enormous feet, and face-planted onto the floor.

Meanwhile, the second Rhunnin, who was missing his front teeth, advanced on Mateo with a wicked smile. "Give up, Earth Boy," said Gaptooth.

"Eat broccoli, alien scum!" cried Mateo, surprising

himself with the bold words. Plucking a hoop from its bracket, he flung it at the man.

Gaptooth batted it away and kept coming. So Mateo threw all the rest of the hoops in his face. Finally the man got his feet tangled on them and fell, landing on his alien butt.

Lucky we didn't run into a coordinated bunch of alien smugglers, thought Mateo.

By this time, Scarface had risen again and was chasing NoWay back and forth between the two rooms. Pennzoil had retreated to his desk, watching the action with a little smile.

"That stinker ratted us out!" cried Booker.

"I—*unh!*—figured that," said Mateo, fending off Crooked Horns with a stilt.

Booker chucked a desktop sculpture at the Pockadoo. It bounced off her head, stunning her. "I think he's working together with the smugglers."

"Uh, yeah," said Mateo. "Same." Sticking out a foot, he tripped Scarface in mid-chase. The alien splashed face-first into the shallow pool.

Jennica snatched up one of the stilts, then whacked Gaptooth with it. Since she was a star softball player, it was a mighty whack. He went down hard. For a moment, all three smugglers were out of commission.

"Let's go!" cried Jennica, dashing for the office door.

The crew fell in behind her. "You're a very bad man!" Tina yelled at Pennzoil as they rushed past.

"But a very good corrupt politician," he said.

Blowing past the little robot outside the door, the team ran full tilt for the elevator. But all that greeted them was a blank wall. Mateo and the others pressed random spots, trying to activate the control panel. Nothing happened.

"Hurry!" cried Tina, glancing back down the hallway. "They'll be here any second!"

Mateo hammered on the wall. "How do you work this thing?"

"Jolly well helping you I can be," said a mechanical voice.

Glancing down, Mateo saw the robot extending its arm. The elevator door snicked open. Everyone piled in.

"Shut the door!" cried Tina. "Now!"

The broccoli smugglers burst out of Pennzoil's office and pounded down the hall toward the elevator. At the sight of the crew, they roared inhuman cries of rage. (Appropriately enough, since they were aliens.)

"Any time now," said Booker.

"Waiting for your friends, should I?" the robot asked.

"NO!" everyone yelled.

Just before the angry Pockadoo reached them, the

elevator door slid shut. Something heavy slammed into it from the other side.

Mateo's heart was hammering so hard he could hear it in his ears. He slumped against a wall, but then a realization brought him upright again.

"Is this the only elevator?" he asked the robot.

"One jolly-jolly elevator, yes!" was the reply.

He blew out a sigh of relief.

A short while later, the elevator door whooshed open. "Again please to be coming," said the robot. "Happy trails wishes you from Pennzoil the Most Groovy!"

But it was addressing empty air. The crew had made a break for it.

As they dove into the hovercraft, Mateo said, "Well, your buddy Grunthar's advice turned out to be pretty lame."

"Why do you say that?" asked NoWay. Clorox elbowed him aside and started the vehicle.

"He sent us to a crooked politician who only pretended to help," said Mateo.

Booker scowled. "Yeah, and he sent us to that science lab where they said they'd never experiment on higher life forms like dogs."

"Maybe Grunthar the Great was confused?" said NoWay.

Tina's glare gave him all the answer he needed.

The hovercraft lifted into the air, and Clorox asked, "Where do we go?"

"The portal!" cried Jennica. "Now!"

"Anywhere but here," said Booker.

"Agreed," said Mateo. "I don't want to know what those smugglers would do to keep their secret safe." But the fact that they hadn't found Elvis ate at his guts like a jalapeño-and-vinegar milkshake.

The craft blasted away from the government complex just as the smugglers came tearing out of the mushroom building. Glancing back, Mateo saw them shouting and shaking their fists. Then the vehicle rounded a dome, and their pursuers disappeared from view.

Mateo's temples throbbed, like that time he'd chugged two slushies on a bet. Several ideas were colliding. He rubbed his forehead.

"Headache?" said Booker.

128

"Nah, it's something . . ." Suddenly it struck him. "*That's* what's been bugging me."

"What?" said Tina. "The fact that alien broccoli smugglers are trying to zap us?"

Mateo shook his head. "No. Back at that lab, remember the scientist told us the TransMog Ray doesn't really make the monsters behave differently?"

"Right," said Booker.

"So then why was the foofaloofa at the lab acting so differently from the one at Grunthar's place?"

NoWay glanced behind them. "Guys? They're following us."

Clorox increased speed. Mateo wanted to focus on the vengeful smugglers behind them, but his mind wouldn't let go of the nagging question. "I mean, they should both act the same, right?"

Jennica twirled a lock of hair. "Grunthar said the one at his place was more like a pet," she mused.

"But even so," said Mateo. "They acted like two different animals."

"Maybe they were," said Booker.

And that's when it hit Mateo. The bad advice, the foofaloofa that wasn't a normal foofaloofa, the TransMog Ray . . .

"It's Grunthar," said Mateo.

"What is?" asked Clorox.

"Go back to his place," said Mateo, sitting bolt upright. "Now!"

"No!" said Jennica. "We're going home."

Clorox swerved left, setting a new course.

The babysitter ground her teeth. "Why does nobody listen to me?"

Tina turned to her brother. "I don't get it."

Spreading his hands, Mateo said, "Don't you see? It all fits together."

"How?"

Mateo ticked off points on his fingers. "First, Grunthar knew we were coming because Nintendo told him. Then he used his TransMog Ray, and finally, he sent us on a wild goose chase."

NoWay frowned. "Goose? There are no gooses on Kroon."

"Figure of speech," said Mateo. "And the reason he did all this is—"

"Because he hates Earthlings?" said Booker.

Suddenly Tina saw it. "Because *he's* got Elvis."

"Disguised as a foofaloofa." Mateo nodded. "He's been there all along."

Tina slammed a fist into her palm. "That major doody-head!"

Checking over his shoulder, Booker said, "They're gaining on us."

Sure enough, the smugglers were growing closer every second. Mateo could just make out Scarface's scowl through the windshield. It wasn't pretty.

Mateo glanced around, searching for a distraction that would slow their pursuers. He couldn't fail now—now that he'd finally cracked the mystery.

A funky smell reached his nostrils, and Mateo grimaced. "Eww, what's that?"

Clorox pointed at a slow-moving hover-truck ahead of them. "It is, how do you say, fertilizing service truck?"

"Full of nookwanda poop," said NoWay.

Something about the situation reminded Mateo of an old movie his parents had showed them. One corner of his mouth curled in a smile.

"Pull up right behind that truck," he said.

"But the smugglers will catch us," said Clorox.

"Not if we play it right," said Mateo. "Um, stay on their bumper and be ready to dive when I say so."

Clorox nodded. She pulled up right behind the truck, near enough so that the smell was almost overwhelming.

Jennica fanned the air. "Sweet fancy Moses!"

"*Pee-yew!*" Booker pinched his nose shut. "If you're wrong, Mateo, that's going to be the last thing we smell in this life."

To settle his fidgeting, Mateo clasped his hands together. He wasn't used to giving orders and coming up with plans. He really hoped this would work.

As Clorox had predicted, the smugglers pulled up right behind them. Angry faces filled the van's windshield. It looked like they were shouting something.

Cupping a hand behind his ear, Mateo cried, "What's that? Can't hear you."

When the smugglers yelled some more, Mateo repeated his gesture. In frustration, Scarface jabbed at his control panel, and the smugglers' windshield retracted.

"I said," Scarface roared, "you learned our secret. We will make you pay!"

Mateo's stomach twisted into a knot. He gulped down his panic, but somehow managed to say, "Ha! I'd like to see you try."

The Rhunnin's face turned the color of a baboon's behind. "I grant your wish," he growled. With that, he backed up his hover-van and gunned it, ramming full speed into the rear of NoWay's vehicle.

Everyone screamed. Their hovercraft hit the back of the fertilizer truck with a serious *KRUNCH!* The truck's tailgate buckled but didn't give.

"My parental units will kill me," moaned NoWay.

"If the smugglers don't do it first," said Booker.

Mateo twisted around to face their pursuers. "Is that all you got?" he yelled.

Eyes nearly popping with rage, Scarface backed up again. When he zoomed forward, Mateo cried, "Now!"

Clorox jerked the controls, sending their craft diving sideways, out of danger.

With nothing to stop it, the hover-van slammed into the fertilizer truck at full speed.

The truck's tailgate gave way.

FWOOMP!

And an entire truckload of nookwanda poop poured through the smugglers' open windshield.

Chapter 15

HIDING IN PLAIN SIGHT

"**Woo-hoo!**" **Tina crowed.** "I can't believe that worked."

Clorox accelerated away from the accident scene. Glancing back, Mateo saw that both vehicles had landed, and the enormous Pockadoo truck driver was cussing out the over-fertilized smugglers.

Tina punched Mateo's shoulder. "Every now and then, bro, you get it right."

"Gee, thanks." But Mateo felt a warm glow.

Maneuvering through the suburbs, Clorox steered their beat-up craft toward Grunthar's volcano lair. Kroon's two suns were dipping low in the sky. Mateo wondered what time it was back on Earth.

Apparently, Jennica was wondering the same thing.

"Hurry up!" she urged Clorox. "If I don't get these kids home before their parents, we're all going to wish we'd stayed inside the chooka-chooka-wee."

Mateo gulped.

"We're almost there," said NoWay. He'd been unusually quiet since hearing his idol get trashed. "I truly hope you're wrong about Grunthar the Great."

"We'll see," Mateo replied grimly.

If he *was* wrong, they'd run out of time. He'd have to return home and leave his dog on this strange planet. And he *really* didn't want to do that.

Soon enough, Grunthar's volcano mansion rose above the warped trees. As they approached, Mateo fretted. *What if Grunthar wouldn't open the volcano hatch? What if he denied everything? How would they get Elvis out?*

His first worry was unfounded. The volcano's hatch gaped wide open. Working the joystick, Clorox set them down gently beside the fountain.

So far, so good.

Before the hovercraft's engines had even shut off, one of Grunthar's Rhunnin assistants came trotting up. He addressed NoWay and Clorox in their alien language. They answered, indicating the Earth kids.

"Sorry," said the assistant in English. "The master is not welcoming visitors now."

Mateo's heart sank. After all they'd been through, the guy wouldn't even talk to them?

"Well, he'd better welcome us," said Tina, jutting out her chin.

The Rhunnin folded his arms. "Come back tomorrow."

Normally Mateo would have backed off, apologized, avoided conflict. But he'd finally reached his limit. His muscles quivered, and his heartbeat thrummed. Like lava rising through his throat, a single hot word erupted: "No!"

The assistant attempted a smile. "But the master—"

"Doesn't need to see us," said Mateo, climbing out of the craft. "I bet I know where he's keeping our dog. Come on, guys!"

And with that, he bounded past the Rhunnin, making for the pink hallway they'd visited last time. The group fell in behind him, passing around the assistant like water around a rock.

"Wait!" the man cried. "You can't just walk in there."

"Seriously?" said Tina. "We're already doing it."

Grunthar's assistant scrambled to get ahead of them. He tried blocking the doorway with spread arms. "Off-limits!"

Ducking underneath, Mateo kept on going. The assistant wavered, torn between fetching Grunthar and trying to stop them.

"If I were you," said Booker as he passed the man, "I'd look for another job."

The Rhunnin sighed. "You might be right. We don't even get dental care."

Mateo felt like he was floating outside his own

body, watching himself take action. Part of him couldn't believe he was doing and saying the things he was doing and saying. It scared him, but it thrilled him, too. Maybe he had a little hero in him after all?

As they hurried down the corridor, Mateo called over and over, "Elvis! Here, boy! Elvis?"

At last, a faint bark echoed from behind a door. Relief flooded him. The crew ran up to the door, and Mateo searched for its control panel.

He pushed and prodded the wall. "How do you open this danged thing?"

"The panel should be somewhere," said Clorox.

Everyone helped, patting the wall while Elvis barked up a storm inside the room. Finally, Tina pressed the right spot, and the panel opened. "Aha!"

She put her hand to the scanner. Nothing happened.

"Why isn't it working?" asked Booker.

NoWay looked like he'd swallowed a lemon. "Maybe only Grunthar's people can open it?"

Hammering on the door, Mateo said, "We've got to get Elvis out of there!" The dog seemed to agree, ratcheting up his barks to the next level.

Footsteps slammed down the hallway. The crew turned to find Grunthar, the assistant, and a Pockadoo bearing down on them.

"Stop that right now!" cried Grunthar. "You can't be in here."

Tina advanced on him. "You lied!"

"Yeah!" said Mateo, joining her. "You told us you'd never even met a dog."

Grunthar's eyes shifted. He didn't seem to know what to do with his hands. "I, uh, haven't."

Elvis barked again.

"Then what's that?" asked Jennica.

Tugging on an earlobe, Grunthar studied the ceiling. "Er, um, a honkadoodle?"

"That's our dog," said Mateo. "Let him out. Now."

"I, er, don't know what you're talking about." The inventor shifted from foot to foot, avoiding their glares.

Booker shook his head. "Man, you are the worst liar I've ever met. My baby sister lies better than you."

Grunthar threw up his hands. "All right, all right! I have your dog."

"I *knew* it!" said Mateo. The others smiled. NoWay looked blue.

"Why did you take him?" asked Tina.

Jennica frowned. "And why didn't you give him back earlier?"

Grunthar crossed to the control panel and then

pressed his palm onto the scanner. The door slid open. Elvis came bounding out to greet them.

Mateo dropped to his knees, hugging the dog as Elvis licked his face. "You sweet knucklehead!" he said, using his dad's favorite nickname for Elvis. "You scared us."

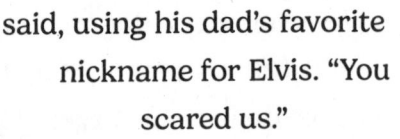

Behind the dog, Mateo could see that all the furniture in the room had been shredded and that the winged elephant seal creature was cowering in the corner. Elvis had made his mark.

"I was only holding him for questioning," said Grunthar. "I was planning on giving him back."

Tina joined Mateo in petting their dog. "Questioning *Elvis*?" she said. "That's the dumbest thing I've ever heard."

"Not even the LingoPop worked." Grunthar slumped. "Your dog speaks a very rare language."

"Sure," said Booker, surveying the wrecked room. "The language of destruction."

Bustling forward, Jennica tugged Mateo and Tina

to their feet. "We're wasting time. We should have left ages ago."

"Not without Elvis," said Mateo.

"I've been more than patient." Jennica nudged her charges along. "We're leaving right now."

Grunthar looked up. "Already? But Elvis wouldn't talk, and I have so much to ask you."

"It'll wait," said Jennica, using her sternest babysitter voice.

The team hustled back down the hallway to their hovercraft, with Elvis frolicking along beside them and Grunthar's posse bringing up the rear. But just as they emerged into the courtyard, they got a nasty shock.

A second hovercraft was landing, a seriously stinky one full of irate smugglers.

"I knew it," said Booker.

"Knew what?" asked Mateo.

Booker shook his head. "Whenever things are looking rosiest, that's when the universe gives you an atomic wedgie."

"You can say that again," said Mateo.

"Whenever things are looking rosiest—" Booker began.

Mateo held up a hand. "On second thought, once is enough."

Chapter 16

STEAMED BROCCOLI

To call the smugglers angry would be a slight understatement. They were going ballistic, they were beyond gonzo, they were throwing a major hissy fit. They were hangry, hot under the collar, fit to be tied, and having kittens.

In short, they were totally ticked off.

Plus, they smelled like nookwanda poop.

As soon as their vehicle touched down, Gaptooth, Scarface, and Crooked Horns boiled out of the van with evil intent. Elvis growled, and his hackles rose.

Mateo's legs felt wobbly. His breath caught in his throat. He and his friends were trapped in an enclosed space with nowhere to run. Was this how it all ended?

"You?" said Gaptooth, gawking at the Earth kids. He looked equal parts confused and annoyed.

Mateo clenched his fists.

But then the smugglers glared past the Earth

kids at Grunthar and his posse.

"You!" Scarface growled. He spat out something in his Rhunnin dialect. Judging by his tone and Grunthar's reaction, Mateo figured it wasn't an alien love poem.

The inventor shouted back, shaking his fist. His flunkies bristled.

"It sounds like they had a business deal with Grunthar," said Clorox.

Booker nodded. "Let me guess. It didn't end well?"

"You could say that," said NoWay.

Roaring with rage, the smugglers charged. The Earth kids and alien teens scrambled out of the way. When the smugglers collided with Grunthar's crew, fists flew and Pockadoos headbutted. Scarface and Grunthar had their hands wrapped around each other's throats, choking out curses.

A sudden giddiness came over Mateo. He almost giggled. It was nice to watch someone else getting attacked for a change.

He felt a tap on his shoulder.

"Now might be a good time to, er . . . ," Clorox whispered, jerking her head toward the hovercraft.

"Make our escape?" whispered Mateo.

"Yes."

Sauntering as casually as possible, the Earth kids

and alien teens drifted toward their vehicle. Mateo even tried to whistle an innocent tune, but his lips were as dry as the Sahara in summer.

Somehow they reached their hovercraft without the smugglers noticing. The crew and Elvis eased inside, and Clorox lifted off. Mateo held his breath. Would the smugglers pursue them?

As it turned out, he needn't have worried. When Gaptooth glanced up and spotted their craft, Grunthar's Pockadoo used the distraction to headbutt him in the belly. The fight raged on.

Up and up their hovercraft went, and when it cleared the volcano's lip, Clorox put the pedal to the metal. Off they zoomed into the Kroonian sunset.

Elvis sat on Mateo's lap, leaning out and sniffing the breeze. Mateo buried his hands in the dog's fur, reveling in the feel of his warm, solid body. A slow grin spread across his face.

They had done it.

They had solved the mystery and found Elvis. And Mateo had been an actual hero.

A bubble of warmth rose within him. Mateo turned to Booker.

"Well, we didn't die a horrible death on an alien planet," he said.

"Yet," Booker replied.

On the other end of the bench seat, Tina gazed out at the strange landscape passing below. The warped, Dr. Seussian trees. The domed houses. The hovercrafts floating along the avenues. Now that they'd finally found Elvis and were headed home, she had a chance to take a breath and appreciate one inescapable fact:

They'd visited an alien world.

And how many kids in her grade could say that?

Before long, the hovercraft approached the park where the portal stood. When he spotted it, NoWay turned to Jennica and the Earth kids. His eyes looked a little misty.

"It was my dream to meet Earth people," he said. "You made my dream come true."

Leaning forward, Jennica kissed his cheek. "We couldn't have done this without you. And Clorox."

The alien girl glanced back at them. "This was adventure of a lifetime."

"It really was," said Mateo.

"I hope we meet again soon and share pizza pie," said Clorox.

Tina leaned closer. "Sure, come visit us anytime. Just . . . don't bring Grunthar, okay?"

"Okey dokey, artichokey," said NoWay. One side of his mouth curved up in a sad smile. "I may have been wrong about him, but I was right about you."

"What do you mean?" asked Jennica.

"From watching your historical records, I always thought Earth people would be chilly."

Mateo quirked an eyebrow. "Chilly?"

"I think he means *cool*," said Clorox.

NoWay nodded. "Cool. And now that I've met you, I know that's true."

Tina scowled. "Don't get all mushy on us." But Mateo could tell she was pleased.

"Mushy?" NoWay tilted his head. "Like an overripe wookaberry?"

Smiling, Mateo said, "Something like that."

When they landed near the portal, the crew noticed something different. Two Pockadoo guards had been posted at the gate in the surrounding fence. And they carried some serious looking ray guns.

"See?" said Booker. "Still a chance for great bodily harm."

When Mateo and the gang walked up to the gate, the guards stood straighter. They called out a challenge in their alien tongue. NoWay gaped in dismay, but Clorox answered them. After some discussion, the taller Pockadoo addressed the Earth kids.

"She say you from Earth," he rumbled.

"Yes, that's right," said Jennica.

The orange alien glowered. "Proof?"

Mateo and the others radiated confusion. "Proof?" he asked.

Resting a thick hand on his holstered ray gun, the guard said, "Some people pretend. But they not real Earth people."

Mateo blew out a sigh. So close, but still so far.

"We're talking an Earth language," he said. "Proof enough?"

The Pockadoo's scowl deepened. "No. Many on Kroon speak Earth language."

Tina tried. "We have an Earth animal with us." She indicated Elvis, who was sniffing the other Pockadoo's leg like he wanted to mark his territory on it.

The first guard shrugged. "Sometimes Earth animals come through."

"Oh, for the love of—" Jennica said. She dug into her jeans pocket, producing her driver's license. "Look, see? My picture. And it's in Earth language."

Taking the laminated card in his huge paw, the taller Pockadoo peered at it suspiciously, then squinted at Jennica. He showed the license to the second guard, who made some comment.

Finally, the first guard handed it back to Jennica. "Okay," he growled. "You go."

The Earth kids sagged in relief.

"But not you," said the Pockadoo, pointing at Clorox and NoWay. They raised their hands in a gesture of surrender.

After some quick hugs from Clorox and high fives

from NoWay, Jennica herded the Earth kids through the gate and up to the portal. "Everyone ready?" she asked, slipping back into babysitter mode.

The three kids nodded. Elvis scratched himself with a hind leg.

And they stepped into the oval of shimmering night sky.

Chapter 17
A COUPLE OF ANGELS

The portal's psychedelic rainbow lights, smeared stars, and incense fragrance didn't seem so strange this time. When the four Earthlings emerged on the other side, it was full dark. Leaves crunched underfoot, and the familiar woodsy smell of home enveloped them.

Through the trees, Mateo could see the lights of Booker's house shining bright, and beyond that, his own house. He let out a breath he didn't know he'd been holding.

They were home at last.

A shove on the shoulder broke his reverie. "Hurry up!" said Jennica. "No dawdling."

Off they marched through the woods. At a fork in the trail, Booker paused before heading down the path to his house. "Nice knowing you."

"What do you mean?" asked Mateo. "We survived."

"Sure, we survived *Kroon*," said Booker.

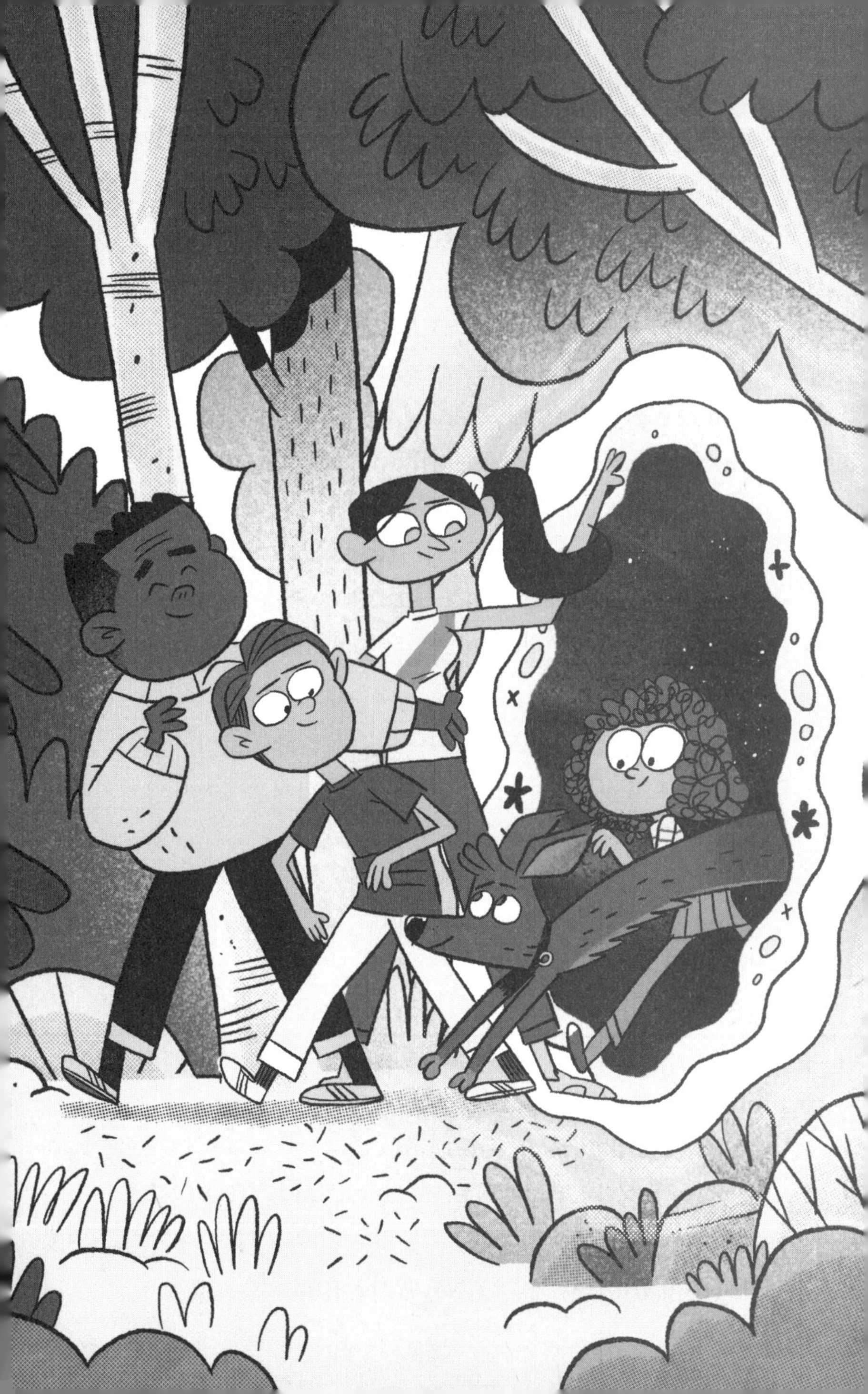

"Meaning?"

Booker grimaced. "My gran will have a cow, and my parents will permanently ground me for coming home late."

"Naw . . ." Mateo couldn't believe it.

"Seriously. See you when we're old. Maybe then we can have a pillow fight. Gently."

Mateo shook his head, smiling. But the smile dropped when reality intruded. If his parents were already home from their date, he and Tina would be in more trouble than a tufted titmouse at a bird-dog convention. Keeping a tight grip on Elvis's collar, he picked up his pace.

The three of them cut through the backyard, crept up to the backdoor, and listened.

Nothing but TV sounds.

"I don't hear any voices," whispered Tina.

"Maybe they're out looking for us," said Mateo. "What time is it?"

Checking her cell phone, Jennica gasped. "Almost nine o'clock?! We're all toast." But just then, her phone pinged with an incoming text.

"Who is it?" asked Tina.

Scanning the message, Jennica said, "Your parents."

Mateo winced. "Are they really mad?"

Jennica shook her head. "They apologized for staying out later than expected. They're headed home."

Tina sagged in relief, but Mateo asked, "Um, when was that text sent?"

"Eight twenty-five."

A cold fist of dread clutched Mateo's insides. "They'll be home any minute. Move it!"

Flinging the door open, Jennica ushered them inside. The squeak of tires on asphalt sounded from the driveway.

"They're here!" cried Tina.

"You two are supposed to be in bed by nine," said Jennica. "Get up there!"

As Jennica vaulted onto the couch in front of the TV, Tina and Mateo pounded up the stairs.

A key rattled in the front door. "We're home!" Mrs. Garcia-Jackson sang out.

No time for niceties. Reaching their own rooms, Mateo and Tina kicked off their shoes and dove under the covers. Elvis hopped onto Mateo's bed and curled up on his feet. It had been a long day for the dog.

Their parents' voices drifted up from below.

"Did they give you any trouble?" asked their father.

"No," said Jennica. "A couple of little angels."

"Hmm," said their mother. "Are you sure you babysat the right house? That doesn't sound like our kids."

Everybody laughed. The conversation quieted, and Mateo heard footsteps on the stairs. He closed his eyes.

When the bedroom door opened, the scent of roses wafted into the room. Mom's perfume. He felt a cool hand brushing his hair back, a soft kiss on his forehead.

"Good night, cariño," said Mrs. Garcia-Jackson.

"G'night, Mom," mumbled Mateo, in what he hoped was a sleepy voice.

She sniffed. "Something smells funny . . . like old-lady perfume and moo shu pork."

Mateo stiffened. How could the smell of Kroon have followed them home? He muttered, "Mmm, moo shu," hoping that would throw her off.

His mother chuckled. She patted his shoulder, then slipped out the door to say good night to Tina.

Later, when his parents had settled down to watch TV in the living room, Mateo heard his door creak open.

"You awake?" whispered Tina.

"After all that?" he answered. "You're kidding, right?"

She crept into the room and sat on the edge of his bed, petting Elvis.

"Wow," said Tina.

"Wow," Mateo agreed, sitting up.

They shared a companionable silence. Then Tina said, "Think we'll ever see those guys again?"

He lifted a shoulder. "Unless they close the portal, we could always go back to visit."

"Yeah." She nodded. "Maybe not right away, though."

"Maybe not."

Another silence. Then Tina said, "You know what's bugging me?"

"What?" said Mateo.

"Grunthar wanted to question Elvis so bad that he dognapped him."

"Yeah?"

Tina frowned. "So what the heck did he want to ask?"

Gazing out the window at the misshapen moon, Mateo said, "We may never know."

Meanwhile, on the other side of the galaxy, in a volcano-shaped mansion, Grunthar and his flunkies were using the Heal-o-Matic to cure their bumps and bruises from the fight. It had taken some fast talking, but he'd finally managed to soothe the smugglers and strike a new deal with them.

"Too bad those kids and their dog got away," said his Rhunnin assistant, Gucci.

Grunthar scoffed. "A minor setback."

"But your plans . . . ?"

"Will still go forward," said the inventor.

"You mean . . . ?"

Grunthar smiled. It wasn't a pretty sight. "Yes. Next step, destination: Earth!"

Gucci shook his head. He chuckled. "They'll never know what hit them."

"No," said Grunthar. "They certainly won't."

Don't miss Mateo, Tina, Booker, and Jennica on their next adventure!

THE OUTER SPACE MYSTERY PIZZA CLUB #2: GRUNTHAR'S REVENGE

OUT NOW!